CHRISTMAS IN CLOVER SPRINGS

CLOVER SPRINGS MAIL ORDER BRIDES

RACHEL WESSON

LONDONGATE PUBLISHING

CHRISTMAS IN CLOVER SPRINGS

CHAPTER 1

TRAIN TO CLOVER SPRINGS, DECEMBER 1886

Alicia Carstairs pushed a blonde hair back from her face as she looked out the train window. The whole landscape was covered in snow. There were no houses or towns for miles, never mind a city. How different it was from Boston, the city of her birth and up till recently her home.

A loud slap followed by a scream broke into her thoughts. She turned away from the window, to see a young boy with the mark of a hand clearly outlined on his face being dragged along the car by a shabbily dressed woman. Furious, she stood up. "Stop."

Surprised, the lady came to a standstill the boy slamming into her legs.

"How dare you hit this child? What did he do to deserve it?" Alicia said, realizing, from the woman's facial expression, her clothes and cultured accent was having an effect.

"What business is it of yours?" the woman replied. However, her eyes were darting left to right as if hoping someone would come to her aid.

"Child cruelty is everyone's business. Why would any mother treat her son so cruelly?"

The woman laughed, a coarse sound. "He's not my son. Him and the rest of the brats are on their way to Leadville."

"Why?"

"They are going to work there. Why do you think?"

"Work, but he's a child?" Alicia looked closer at the boy who had stopped crying. His big blue eyes were focused on her. "He is only about seven or eight. What sort of job would he do?"

"The mines need children."

Horrified, Alicia opened and closed her mouth a couple of times. "The mines? You cannot mean that this child is going to be working underground. It's too dangerous."

"It's none of your business." The male voice made the hairs on the back of her neck rise. She hadn't noticed the rough looking man moving toward them. "Go back to your seat and leave us alone."

She turned to go back to her seat but a glance at

the boy stopped her. He wasn't making a sound but his eyes were pleading for help.

"I will not. I demand to know by whose authority you are taking this child to Leadville. Where are his parents?" Alicia was glad her voice wasn't shaking despite the trembling in her legs.

"Listen, miss, he's an orphan. He ain't got no parents. The orphanage signed him and the others into my care. So stay out of it." The man's tone combined with his menacing glare should have been enough to make Alicia sit back down. Instead it had the opposite effect. She guessed he was acting so belligerently because he had something to hide. She wasn't about to leave the boy with him until she was satisfied the child would be alright.

"Others. You mean there are more?" Alicia addressed the man, but seeing his face close in anger, she decided he'd probably realized he had said enough.

Alicia bent down and spoke directly to the child. "Why are you traveling with these people? Tell me please. I want to help you."

The little boy looked at her for a couple of seconds before saying,

"Matron said they were taking us to new homes. We would get a new ma and pa. All of us. I think she was lying. She said we would get food on the train and we ain't had nothing to eat for days," the boy hiccuped.

"I went looking for some food when she wasn't looking. Didn't get far enough. She caught me."

"Oh you poor child." Alicia reached into the basket she had brought with her. She took out her breakfast, a sandwich, and hurriedly wrapped it up in a napkin before giving it to the boy. "Here, take this."

"Thank you, ma'am. Hey, you're not looking for two children are you? I have a younger brother, he can't talk. I'd work hard enough to keep both of us and we'd both go to school." The expression on his face at the mention of school amused her although she didn't show it. She didn't get a chance to answer.

"A lady like her ain't interested in a brat like you."

Alicia had to move out of the way quickly as the woman pushed past her, dragging the boy behind her. The man followed, giving Alicia a dirty look.

Sitting down, she couldn't relax. Just how many children were on their way to Leadville? What would happen to them once they got there? Why would anyone trust a pair like that with one child never mind more? *It's not your concern. You have enough problems of your own. Yes, but if someone had come to help me, I wouldn't be sitting here. Alone.*

CHAPTER 2

Closing her eyes, Alicia tried to distract herself by thinking of her own perilous situation. She'd never been a governess before. Would she meet Mr. Oaks expectations? Robert seemed to think so. Alicia opened her eyes. Robert was the last person she wanted to think about.

Why are you sitting here when a child or children could be in trouble? You could easily check on the boy. All you have to do is walk into the next car. There can't be that many children traveling to Leadville. Maybe she could take the boy and his brother and bring them to meet Mr. Oaks. He may be able to help them avoid the mines. He was a father himself.

Alicia gave up arguing with herself. She couldn't just sit there. She had to go find out how many children there were and why. Taking her carpetbag, she moved down the car following in the direction of the woman. She hadn't gone that far when she spotted a priest. Maybe he would help her. Wouldn't hurt to have him accompany her. She wasn't a coward but the rough looking man who had told her to mind her own business looked dangerous.

"Excuse me, Father, but I wondered if I might have a word?"

"Of course, please sit down."

Alicia sat and took a minute to arrange her skirts.

"My name is Father Molloy." The priest smiled as he extended his hand.

"Alicia Carstairs, Father," she replied, shaking his hand.

"Are you traveling alone, Miss Carstairs?"

Alicia nodded but before the priest started asking personal questions, she asked, "Father, did you notice a woman and a child coming through the car a little while ago?"

"No, I can't say I did. I might have been in the dining car though. These three boys get mighty hungry. He pointed at the children sitting on the seats on the other side of the carriage. Alicia hadn't noticed them. They looked a little like the boy she had spoken to only their clothes were cleaner. Was the priest involved in taking the children to Leadville too? Surely not. But maybe it had been a mistake to stop to speak to him.

"Sorry, Father, I didn't mean to disturb you. I will let you get back to your reading."

"Miss, please tell me what is troubling you. I can see you are distressed."

Alicia stared into his eyes. He looked kind. She sensed she could trust him.

"I met a child a while ago. A woman had just hit him across the face. She says he's an orphan on his way to work in Leadville, in the mines."

The priest straightened in his seat. "The mines? Children?"

"Yes, Father. This boy was only about seven or eight. I gave him a sandwich but from what he says, none of the children with him have had anything to eat for some time. I can't think of what type of people would allow children to travel with the adults I met."

"Unfortunately, it is becoming more and more common. We simply cannot cope with the number of orphans in the cities. The authorities made arrangements for them to be sent west where there should be more opportunities."

"Opportunities for what? To be treated like animals and left to die. I won't stand for that. It is not right."

Alicia's indignation raised her tone causing people around them to look up. She flushed. She wasn't used to being the center of attention.

"It certainly isn't. Why don't you sit here and mind my boys while I go and see what the situation is?"

"Sorry, Father, but I can't let you go alone." The man was nasty enough to strike an old man even if he was a priest.

His eyebrows rose as he looked to her for an explanation.

"Sorry, Father, I don't mean to be rude, but you haven't seen these people. The man, well he looks dangerous. I think its best if we both go."

"Perhaps we should also bring the conductor. If they do make trouble, he may be able to help us."

As it turned out, the conductor wasn't around. Alicia followed the priest down the car and into the next one. She couldn't believe her eyes. There were at least thirty children of all ages sitting in the carriage. Some were openly crying, others looked shocked into silence. None were laughing or joking as you would expect children that young to behave. Miserable and scared, they didn't even look up but stared at the ground or out the window. The woman she had seen earlier was sitting down eating a sandwich. She recognized the napkin. *That's my breakfast.*

Without thinking Alicia marched up to the woman, snatching the sandwich from her hand. "I gave my breakfast to the child. Not to you."

The woman started coughing as the food went down the wrong way.

"We told you to leave it alone. Go back to your seat if you know what's good for you." The man was so close to her, his spittle landed on her face. Disgusted, she removed it with her hanky.

"I do not take orders from the likes of you. I want to see the documents you hold giving you the authority to take these children to Leadville." Alicia smiled to herself as she saw the fear flare in his eyes. Being the daughter of a lawyer had its advantages.

"Documents?" The man said looking at her blankly.

"Legal documents." Alicia looked down her nose at him. "The papers the judge gave you so you could take the children across state lines."

"P—paperwork. I don't have any. But these kids are mine and are staying with me." His aggressive tone didn't frighten her. Instead, she was more convinced she had to get the children away from him.

"We shall have to disagree about that. Section five of the Children's Act states that all minor children traveling with someone other than a parent, across state lines, must hold the correct documentation."

Alicia hoped the man would think her cheeks were flushed with temper rather than guilt for telling lies.

"As is required by law, every one of these children must be able to show they are part of your group. Otherwise...*sir,* you can and will be charged with kidnapping."

The man's eyes bulged out of his head.

"Kidnapping is a serious offense in this part of the country," the priest added. Only Alicia saw the wink he gave her.

"I don't know nothing about papers. I was told to take these brats to Leadville and leave them there. I ain't going to prison for no-one." The woman's voice trembled with a combination of fear and temper.

"You would be lucky if the penalty wasn't more severe than prison," Alicia murmured.

The woman put a hand to her neck before turning on the rough looking man. "You never said nothing about landing in jail. I ain't going to swing for anyone. I'm through. I'm not having anything to do with these kids. Not for any number of dollars." The woman gathered her meager possessions together putting them into a carpet bag.

"Shut up, May. Can't you see she's bluffing you?"

May used the bag she was packing to hit the man.

"You don't tell me to shut up. You don't know nothing about the law. Look at her. Look at the way she's dressed. She's rich and educated. She wouldn't say something unless it were true."

With that, the woman moved out of the car.

Alicia held the man's gaze. She was glad her dress was covering her shaking legs. She couldn't let this man sense weakness. Not now.

"I would like to see your papers too, sir." The priest echoed.

"I told you. I ain't got no papers. I was just told to take these bra... children to Leadville. I was acting out of the goodness of my heart, them being too young to travel alone. I couldn't afford to feed them. I ain't eaten myself for days." The man ignored Alicia, instead choosing to appeal to the priest.

Alicia hardened her stare.

"Look, why don't you take them. You're a priest. You'll know what to do with them. I can head back to my own place without feeling guilty at leaving these poor kids alone."

"I think that's an excellent solution. As a member of the clergy, Father..." Alicia bit her lip. She couldn't remember his name.

"Molloy," the priest murmured.

"Thank you. As I was saying, as a member of the clergy, Father Molloy doesn't require paperwork. The courts have made allowances for the church to move children in their care. They know the church aims to find proper homes for the orphans." Alicia crossed her fingers.

"See it all worked out in the end. Such a relief to get rid of them. Good day, Father. Miss." The man would have doffed his cap if he was wearing one before following hastily in the footsteps of his friend May.

CHAPTER 3

Alicia sat down with a bump. Her whole body was shaking. She couldn't believe she had fooled the man.

"Miss Carstairs, if I hadn't seen it for myself, I would never have believed a young girl like you could behave with such arrogance." Father Molloy beamed. "Could you stay here for a couple of minutes? I want to get my other charges and bring them up here. I don't like leaving them alone for long."

Alicia wasn't capable of speech so nodded.

"I won't be long." With that, the priest left. She was alone with the children.

Alicia sat on the seat taking deep breaths to try to stop the shaking. She wanted to cry but that wouldn't do. She would only scare her audience who now all seemed to be staring at her.

"Excuse me, miss, but are they really gone?"

The boy she had helped earlier asked as he made his way over to where she sat. He jumped up onto the seat beside her, taking her hand and rubbing it. A flood of feelings overwhelmed her. The child was trying to comfort her.

"Thank you. I don't know for certain but I hope so."

"You some sort of lawyer? You used a lot of big words."

Alicia smiled at an older girl who asked the question. Before she could answer, the boy sitting beside her said, "She ain't a lawyer. She's an angel. My ma told me, I had a guardian angel who would look after me. She said it just before she died so it was true."

"Don't be stupid, Harry, angels don't exist."

"Yes they do." Harry looked up at Alicia, adoration in his face.

"Sorry, Harry, I am not an angel." *Far from it.*

SHE WAS SAVED from doing any more talking by the return of Father Molloy. The conductor followed him. Father Molloy must have told him the story as he was carrying some food and water. Alicia moved to help him. There wasn't enough to give everyone a big meal but at least all the children got to eat something.

. . .

ALICIA EXCUSED herself to return to her seat and collect the rest of her belongings consisting of a coat and a book. She returned to find the children playing games and laughing. The change in them was quite astonishing.

Father Molloy walked toward her, a big smile on his face. "Amazing what a little bit of kindness does for children, isn't it?"

Alicia smiled, although the sight of the children playing brought a lump to her throat.

"Quite a resourceful young lady, aren't you?" The priest's tone was kind but his eyes were inquisitive.

She didn't know what to say to that so let him continue.

"Personally, I have never heard of the Children's Act." Father Molloy's eyes twinkled.

"Sorry, Father, I shouldn't have lied, but I had to do something. I couldn't let these children go with that pair."

"I think in the circumstances your actions were appropriate." Father Molloy, seeing her confusion, continued. "I do not agree with lying, but given the alternatives, I think God would understand. Now, my dear, let's sit down and try and work out what we are going to do with all of these children."

"We, Father?"

"Well, I was hoping you would be able to help.

Unless of course you have pressing business in Denver."

Alicia looked at her hands. She should say no and continue on her journey to Leadville to meet Mr. Oaks. But she didn't want to go to Leadville. She knew nobody there. She had been praying for a miracle. Maybe this was it? Not a miracle but at the very least a way of delaying traveling on alone.

She looked into the priest's face wondering if he would want her if he knew her background. He seemed to sense her indecision as he continued speaking in a more persuasive tone.

"It would only be for a couple of days. I have somewhere to take the children. I can do it myself but the journey would be much more pleasant if you came along too. Then you could continue your trip if my plan doesn't inconvenience you too much."

Alicia squeezed her hands together. She wished her stomach would stop fluttering. She had hated spending Thanksgiving alone and wasn't looking forward to spending Christmas in a strange town working for strangers. Maybe she could spend Christmas with these children. She could telegraph Mr. Oaks. Was she just putting off the inevitable, or could this be an opportunity for a fresh start? Going to Leadville seemed even less attractive than before now that she knew May and that man were going there. She decided to take a chance.

"No, Father, a few days' delay won't matter. Where are we headed? Denver?"

"We will change trains at Denver. My friends live in a town called Clover Springs. They built a new orphanage there during the summer."

"So the children will have somewhere to stay?"

"They will, although it may be a bit of a squeeze."

"Given the alternative on offer, I don't think they will mind, do you?" Alicia smiled at the priest as the sound of children laughing filled the car.

CHAPTER 4

CLOVER SPRINGS DECEMBER 1886

Aaron rode down the track to his homestead. He still couldn't believe this piece of land was his. Well, it would be in five years' time when he had fulfilled the requirements of the Homestead Act.

He'd been blessed to file the claim in the summer. The long hot days had allowed him time to get the frame of the house built and a small barn raised. He could be living here with Asha now if their marriage had gone ahead. After he had gotten over his pride, he was glad he hadn't married Asha. He didn't love her and repaying a debt was not a good reason to get married. *Is marrying a mail order bride a better one?*

Asha and Little Beaver were happy as they waited for the baby to be born. They had built a small lodge on the edge of Frank's homestead. Little Beaver and his wife Asha, being Indians, weren't allowed to file a claim. It was funny how the law had no problem employing Little Beaver to keep the town safe, but it didn't want him to be able to build property.

Aaron didn't want to think about the inequalities his friends faced every day. Instead he was determined to be thankful for the good things they shared. He dismounted in front of the house taking the burlap bag his ma had given him. He tied his horse to the rail making sure the trough had clean water before making his way up the two steps. Opening the door, he put the bag on the table and tried to see the house as his new bride would see it. *If anyone ever answers my letters.*

It looked slightly more cheerful after his ma's last visit. His ma and the other ladies had made him a couple of things for his new home. Two braided rag rugs took pride of place on the floors. They had made some curtains for the windows. He wondered if his new wife would be happy with them. Maybe he should have just left the glass and waited for his wife to put her finishing touches to their home.

The stove he'd ordered hadn't arrived yet but the shelves Paul Kelley had made were a good start to the kitchen area. Sighing he picked up the bag from the table to put the canned foods onto the empty shelves. You would think his wife was due tomorrow given the amount of cans his ma had packed.

Ma believed in being prepared. She didn't know if his mail order bride would bring anything with her. She had left a couple of plates and cups as well as two cast-iron pots and a frying pan for the kitchen and bed linen and towels on her last visit. He noticed she had stored some of his old clothes in the chest of drawers she had donated to what would become the bedroom.

His eyes moved to the large bed in the corner of the main room. Paul was coming over on Saturday. They would put up a dividing wall to separate the bedroom from the rest of the house. His new bride would need her privacy, at least for the first few weeks, until they got to know one another. He rubbed his hands on his pants. It wasn't just for her benefit. He wasn't much good with women. Always said the wrong thing. Usually he made them laugh but often he was the butt of the joke. He wished he had Samuel's way of speaking. Even when he had his stutter, his brother had a better command of the English language. Now he spoke real nice, possibly as he was surrounded by women all the time rather than grumpy old ranchers. Maybe Ma could give me lessons on how to talk to a lady real nice like. Instantly, he dismissed the idea. He loved his ma but she was bound to get Miss Mary and the rest of the ladies involved.

He looked around the cabin. It looked better than it

had a couple of weeks back but would his new wife like it? What if you don't find a bride? What if no one wants to marry you?

Come what may, he was determined to start building up his own homestead. He loved Davy Sullivan and was grateful to the whole Sullivan clan, but it was time he lived on his own land.

He wandered outside taking in the beauty of his surroundings. The mountains to the back provided shelter from the worst of the winds. The creek running along the boundary of his property would provide plenty of clean water.

Davy had agreed to lend him the funds to stock the farm since filing the claim had taken all of his savings on top of a loan from Davy. He figured he would buy some hens, two pigs and a couple of head of cattle.

Despite his decision to keep his thoughts light, he couldn't help but worry about how he would repay his friend. He knew Davy liked to help but it didn't mean it didn't rankle. He hated being in debt to other people. But the reality was, with the current fall in beef prices combined with the summer drought and bad winter, he was lucky to have a friend with money to spare. Too many people were struggling to keep their heads above water. Children were going hungry. It wasn't just children either. There was evidence to suggest the animals were having a hard time too.

Was this the wrong time to settle down? Would his new wife be able to live the life of a homesteader? You told her all about the homestead in your letter. Nobody is going to come out here expecting a fine house and servants.

He checked the homestead one last time, making a note of what he needed to fetch from town, before he mounted his horse and headed back to the Sullivan ranch. Really, he should stop at the store to check if there was any post even though his letter had probably just arrived in Boston. He needed to have a little patience, but it was hard to be patient when feeling lonely.

He wanted to be as happy as his brother and their friends. Although Samuel's case was different. He had known his wife, Ellen, since she was a young girl. But Davy and Mary were happy and they'd married as strangers. Brian and Sorcha were another happy mail order couple.

Whistling, he let his horse make her own way home. He wondered what type of girl would answer his ad. He'd like someone from a big family or an orphan from the same place his friends' wives came from. Someone who understood his need to be around other people. Not all the time but at special occasions like Thanksgiving, Christmas and birthdays. Or when someone decided they wanted to throw a party. His family and friends were important to him, so his wife would have to understand that.

Despite wanting to farm his land, he wouldn't be able to spend all the time on his homestead. He didn't have sufficient savings to build up a herd, or plant enough crops. He would have to go on cattle drives to earn cash. His wife would have to be used to living on a farm and fending for herself. He smiled, thinking of Ellen. He loved his brother's wife but they were lucky they could live in town. Ellen was so squeamish she couldn't skin a dead animal, never mind go out and kill a live one. She had many other assets but a rancher's wife was not in her makeup.

Thinking of his friends made him wonder if he should have highlighted the mixture of nationalities living in Clover Springs. There weren't many towns with an Indian for a deputy sheriff. Father Molloy said some people back East were still afraid of Indians. The girls had told him stories about the hatred they had endured simply because they were Irish. Why couldn't people just learn to live with each other? It was hard enough out here in the West without fighting prejudice too. Aaron Higgins, if your ma could read your thoughts, she would tell you to stop inviting trouble. Your new bride hasn't arrived yet, and you're already worrying about how she will fit into the town.

CHAPTER 5

TRAIN TO CLOVER SPRINGS

The children ate again later before settling down to sleep. Father Molloy checked every one of them before making his way back to where she sat.

It took him a while to find a comfortable position. Alicia knew how he felt. The hard seats on the train seemed to get harder with every hour of their never ending trip. She'd lost count of the number of times they had been delayed due to the weather.

"So, are you studying the law, Miss Carstairs?"

"Me? No. Not at all." A lady lawyer? How her father would laugh when she told him. But she couldn't.

"Pity. You obviously have the mind for it. So where are you headed? Home?"

Alicia wasn't sure how to get away from his questions without being rude. He waited in silence for her reply.

"No my home is in Boston. Or at least it was. I am headed to Leadville too. I have accepted a position as governess to a young family."

"How wonderful. What is the name of the family? Perhaps I have met them?"

"Oaks. I exchanged correspondence with Mr. Oaks. Mrs. Oaks is confined to bed following an accident and they have three young children." Alicia wondered why her story would make the priest look uncomfortable. Was it because she had accepted a position as governess for a family she hadn't met?

"I am sure the Oaks family could survive without your services for a few more days," Father Molloy said firmly. "You will be able to send a telegram from Clover Springs. I don't think it would be prudent for us to waste any time in Denver. May and her friend may return."

Alicia couldn't help feeling the priest had recognized the name of the family, yet he didn't say so. You are just being fanciful because of the experience with May and her friend. They had been lucky to get one over that pair, she didn't fancy her chances if they came back. "Agreed, Father. As I said, I am in no hurry."

. . .

The train change at Denver passed off without incident. Soon they were on their way to Clover Springs.

"Is your parish in Clover Springs, Father?" Alicia asked hoping if she engaged in conversation her stomach would stop roiling with nerves.

"Lord no, but it might as well be." At Alicia's confused expression, the priest explained. "Many of the ladies now living in Clover Springs came from the orphanage attached to my parish in Boston. The town was nice before the girls arrived but it's now even nicer. They came out as mail order brides and each one helps the other. A friendlier place you would be hard-pressed to find."

Alicia wondered how a town could be so pleasant. Maybe because it was smaller than a city. Or was it just because these girls knew each other growing up.

"Father, these ladies you spoke of. You know the mail order wives? Are they happy?" Alicia didn't know what it was about the priest that made her ask. Mama would be horrified at my asking about feelings. Marriage was a business relationship, nothing more and nothing less. It was her duty as a wife to obey her husband. Yet Mama had been lucky. Her father had adored her mother.

"Absolutely. Katie, she's from Ireland, she had a lucky escape. Her original fiancé was part of a gang that robbed the train she was on. Her husband rescued her and they now have two children, a girl and a boy. Mary, Mary Sullivan as she is now, married Katie's brother-in-law. I think Sorcha was next but there have been so many, I get a little confused." The priest laughed at himself.

"Did all the girls come from Ireland?" Alicia did her best to hide her distaste. She hadn't met any Irish people in Boston but her father had told her lots of stories. None of them pleasant.

"Yes, some from the orphanage attached to my parish. The others came a more circular route. Emer, she came to Boston looking for her sister Sorcha, but Sorcha had already left for Clover Springs. Emer followed, the Shipley family was traveling to Denver and she accompanied them. Don't think anyone expected her and Lawrence to marry but they are now the proud parents of twins."

Lawrence Shipley? It couldn't be the same man could it?

"Did they return to live in Boston?" Alicia tried but failed to keep the hopeful note out of her voice.

"Why no, not at all. Lawrence is a very valued member of the Clover Springs community. Once people arrive in Clover Springs they tend not to leave. The town is a special place." Father Molloy regarded her silently.

She was tempted to ask him why, but years of

being taught how ladies were expected to behave prevented her.

"You might find you don't want to leave Clover Springs either."

"I doubt that Father." *You won't want me to stay if your friend Shipley tells you my story.*

Alicia turned her face to the window. Even now, miles away, her former life was casting its shadow on her future.

As the time passed, Alicia ended up learning a lot about the children in her care. Matilda, who preferred to be called Tilly, was fourteen and had lost her mother and father in a house fire. Her younger brothers and sisters had died too. She was saved as she was out getting things at the store. She had been told a family in Leadville wanted her to come to work as a maid. Given her looks and the attitude of May and her friend, Alicia couldn't help feeling Tilly had a lucky escape.

The other children all had similar stories. They had lost parents in various tragedies, although some of them had no memories of their parents. Harry's younger brother, Steven, broke her heart. He didn't speak. Nobody including Harry seemed to know why. He could have been born mute or stopped speaking at some later stage. He was a beautiful child with blond hair and big blue eyes. He liked to listen to her stories so he wasn't deaf. He had taken to sitting on her lap and despite her misgivings, she couldn't stop him. Harry sat at her side, holding her hand tightly as if she would disappear.

DESPITE HER BEST INTENTIONS, the orphans were breaking down the shield around her heart, a little bit more every day. They loved playing with her or listening to her stories. At first, she had struggled to find games to play with them, but it soon became apparent they were easily pleased. The younger ones liked games and stories. The older boys amused themselves most of the time by telling each other ghost stories. The girls liked talking about clothes and fashion. A couple of them, Tilly included, loved to listen to her talk about the social life in Boston. She told them stories of her grandmother being presented at Court in front of Queen Victoria prior to her marrying her grandfather, a plantation owner in the Deep South.

. . .

SHE KNEW she should try to keep a distance from the children. It would only make leaving them behind much harder. She wasn't sure her heart could handle any more heartbreak. Everyone she loved left her. Her parents. Robert. She squeezed her eyes shut determined not to shed any more tears over him. He must have cared as he was the one who'd arranged the governess position with Mr. Oaks. But he didn't care enough to marry you. Not once the scandal broke. She could still hear his voice as he explained why they couldn't get married. *His career would never recover if he married the daughter of a ...*

"Want to play?" Harry asked her, interrupting her thoughts. Harry and his brother Steven were the children she felt closest to. She wasn't being fair to them either. They had already lost their parents, so she shouldn't be letting them form a bond with her. It was better he didn't become even more attached to her.

"Go back to the other children. I have a headache." Alicia said more sharply than she intended, her tone causing Harry to blink in surprised hurt. Father Molloy glanced her way with raised eyebrows. She felt even worse when Harry went back to the other children, his shoulder slumped, his body crying rejection.

It was better this way. The sooner Harry learnt you couldn't trust anyone the better.

CHAPTER 6

In an effort to distract herself, she asked about Clover Springs.

"Who works at the orphanage, Father?"

"Samuel and his wife Ellen Higgins run the orphanage with help from Wilma."

"Only three staff, is it not very big then?"

"No, currently there are only two children living there. Rosa and John, brother and sister. I brought them out from Boston some time back."

Alicia wondered if she should voice her fears or remain silent. Her mother had told her over and over that men did not like a woman who was too opinionated.

"Why are you so silent, Alicia. You seem miles away. Is there anything you would like to talk about?"

"I was just wondering why the children were still

living at the orphanage. I mean you said earlier you would try and find homes for these ones but if you can't find homes for two..." She stopped talking at the look of pain crossing his face "I am sorry, Father, my mother told me often enough I am too outspoken."

"You are an intelligent girl. You are right to be curious. John and Rosa haven't found a suitable home yet. I am hopeful they will but... Well, let's just say the children in our care might be easier to place."

"Are they handicapped?"

"Rosa and John's father was black and their mother is white. A lot of people will not accept children from a mixed background."

"They certainly don't belong in a white home." Alicia could have bit her tongue at the look of disapproval she received.

"I thought you might be different, Miss Carstairs. You have the intelligence to think for yourself, you have a good heart otherwise you wouldn't have intervened when you saw Harry being abused. Yet, you say something like that."

"Like what, Father? There are reasons why we should keep things separate. White children belong with white parents. They should not be adopted by anyone of color be they negro or heavens forbid Indian. White people are superior for a reason. They are more intelligent, more likely to succeed in life and have the ability to provide a decent home." She stopped talking. The man beside her was furious, and she sensed he was trying hard not to lose his temper.

"Those types of opinions are not welcome in Clover Springs. Wilma, the lady who helps run the orphanage, is an ex-slave. Our deputy sheriff is an Indian."

Alicia couldn't help it, her mouth hung open in shock. Someone was having a very good laugh at her expense. It seemed she was heading to a town full of Irish, blacks and Indians. Whatever would people think? *What people? Those who turned their backs on you as soon as the news broke.* She shook her head to get rid of that voice.

"But you can't mean to put these children in the care of those people?"

"I do mean to. You saw how badly they were treated by white folk. Wasn't that sufficient to convince you a person's nature is not determined by the color of their skin." Father Molloy stood up. "Quite frankly, Miss Carstairs, I must go for a walk before I lose my temper completely. I am very disappointed a woman of your intelligence and integrity should hold those opinions."

With that he was gone, leaving her staring after him. She couldn't believe an ex-slave and an Indian held positions of authority in this town they were heading to. Didn't anyone out West read the newspapers. The Indians wanted to murder the whites. Everyone knew the blacks lacked intelligence and were lazy. And the town was full of Irish people. He's Irish. Yes, well a lot of priests were, but that was different. They didn't sit around all day drinking and fighting.

She sat back in her seat, her temper boiling. How dare he chastise her. She was doing him a favor. She should be on her way to Leadville not some town with mixed up views. *Leadville being such a nice place, the employment of children in dangerous jobs is allowed.*

Father Molloy was gone for ages. She shifted about in her seat feeling more uncomfortable. She liked the older man, having only realized when speaking to him how much she missed intelligent conversation. Her father, while not agreeing with her ambition to be a lawyer, used to speak to her a lot about his work. They used to discuss cases. He told her everything. Well, so she thought. Actually, he had left a lot out. He only told her what he wanted her to know.

She closed her eyes trying to sleep but her mind was too busy. Opening them again she saw Harry staring at her. She turned away feeling guilty at hurting the child. "That true what you said?" he whispered.

"You shouldn't have been listening to adult conversations. It's rude."

"I couldn't help it, you were loud." He bit his lip. "Is it true what you said? That you hate black people."

"I never said I hated them. I just believe white people..."

"Are better. Which means you hate them. I think I was wrong. You ain't an angel is you?"

"Harry I told you I wasn't an angel." Alicia tried to be patient but failed dismally.

"Yeah I know, but I thought you were. But angels come from God and he said we had to love everyone. So you can't be an angel if you don't like people just cause of their skin color." The child's face was twisted in anger.

"Harry, go back to sleep. You don't know what you are talking about." Alicia said firmly.

"Yes I do. When Ma died, her friend Opal looked after me and Steven. She wanted to keep us but the men who came said she couldn't 'cause she was black. She cried when they took us away." Harry gulped. "But she cared for us real good. She gave us food and hugs and all. She was a really kind lady not one who just pretended to be. I hate you."

Alicia stared at the boy in shock, tears welling up in her eyes. Looking up, she saw Father Molloy watching her, a look of sadness in his eyes. Angry he had witnessed her weakness she turned away and looked out the window.

"Out of the mouths of babes," he whispered. "Good night, Miss Carstairs. I will pray God sends you enlightenment."

* * *

THE NEXT MORNING, she tried to speak to Harry but he wouldn't acknowledge her. Every time she came near, he turned his back. Surprised she found she missed him, missed his little hand creeping into hers.

Father Molloy brought her breakfast. "Please keep your opinions to yourself when we reach Clover Springs. I am very grateful to you for your help with these children. I admire your honesty and integrity when you stood up for Harry and refused to let the children be sent to Leadville. But I cannot allow you to voice opinions to hurt my friends."

She didn't answer. She wasn't able to.

The train journey dragged on for four more days due to the weather.

"If this keeps up, we are going to spend Christmas on the train," Matilda, said.

"We will get to Clover Springs in time for Christmas. I made a promise to my girls I would be back and I never break promises." Father Molloy smiled brightly but Alicia could see he was concerned too. She wondered if it was wise to raise the children's spirits, but she wasn't about to criticize him. They were back to speaking civilly to one another but not as friendly as before.

"Next stop Clover Springs." The conductor called as he wandered through the car. This was it. Now she would find out whether Clover Springs was a magical place like Father Molloy seemed to think. Whatever it was, she wouldn't be staying. They would ask her to leave as soon as Lawrence Shipley told them her story.

No point thinking about that now. The main thing was to get these children to a warm place where they could have some decent food, a warm bath and a good night's sleep.

CHAPTER 7

CLOVER SPRINGS

"Miss Wilma, Father Molloy is back and he got loads of kids with him. Hundreds." John ran in, his excitement making his eyes light up.

Wilma crossed herself as John ran back outside. Hundreds? Where on earth would they put all them children? How did Father Molloy manage to collect so many? No point in you waiting here to find out, you got to get to the train station.

"Miss Ellen, did you hear John shouting?" Wilma called.

"Yes, Wilma, but I couldn't make out what he was saying. Something about children?" Ellen walked slowly into the kitchen.

Wilma handed her a ginger cookie. It helped keep

the nausea at bay. Ellen was suffering badly with her pregnancy.

"Yes, Miss Ellen. Father Molloy done bring hundreds of children on the train. That's what he said."

"Hundreds." Ellen sat down in a chair, fanning herself despite the bitterly cold wind blowing in the open door. "Hundreds?"

"You stay here, Miss Ellen." Wilma knew the sickness every morning was taking its toll on Ellen. She wouldn't rest as she kept saying she had the carol concert and Christmas pageant to organize. "I got to go see how many children that old priest brought us. How he thinks we going to feed all them young'uns."

Wilma kept speaking to herself as she made her way toward the train station. She saw a crowd forming a little ahead of her and then she heard it. Singing. A lot of children singing. The crowds parted like Moses parting the Red Sea and there was Father Molloy. John hadn't been lying when he said he had brought loads of children. There wasn't a hundred but it sure was a lot of them.

Father Molloy marched up the street leading his little group. He nodded to people he recognized on either side of the street. When he spotted Wilma, his face lit up with a big smile. She waited for him, hands on hips. Not least, as she couldn't get her feet to move.

The sound of the children's voices brought back memories of other young'uns singing their fear away through the hot summer night. Despite the fact she was standing in Colorado in the midst of winter, she could feel the sweltering heat, the mosquitos biting at her skin while the children sang. She wanted to turn and run. Escape from this reminder of her past, but her eyes were glued to those of Father Molloy. He looked haggard, so much older than during the summer. Something bad had happened. He needed help and so did those poor little lambs he led behind him.

"What's going on, Wilma? Where are all those kids going?" Aaron Higgins scratched his hair, his gaze like that of the whole town on the parade marching toward them.

"Father Molloy done come back just like he said he would. Those children are for Hope House."

"What? All of them? Where you going to put them?"

"Never mind about that now, Mr. Aaron. Don't you have better things to be doing than standing around in the street?"

"Ma sent me to ..." Aaron's voice stopped. His eyes widened as he blinked them shut a couple of times as if not believing what he was seeing. Wilma followed his gaze to a point behind Father Molloy toward the rear of the convoy. A tall blonde-haired girl walking in the middle of two young children, holding their hands. She was rather overdressed for Clover Springs. She had one of them fancy bustle things Miss Ellen had worn for college. Wilma watched as the girl stared directly ahead, eyes not turning left or right, as if she was unaware her group was the focus of the town's attention.

For some reason, the girl's attitude annoyed her. It was as if she felt she was too good for their town.

"Isn't she amazing?" Aaron whispered his eyes fixed on the girl.

"You best shut your mouth or you'll catch flies," Wilma said irritably. "Go on now, your ma is waiting on you."

"Wilma, aren't you a sight for sore eyes," Father Molloy's Irish lilt broke into their conversation. "Excuse me, Aaron, isn't it? I must speak with Wilma immediately. It is a matter of urgency."

"Seems to me you should have started speaking to me a few towns back. Could you have not sent a telegram to warn me? How you expect me to feed and shelter all these children? I ain't no miracle worker." Wilma had her hands on her hips as she let the priest know he had messed up.

Father Molloy smiled his sweetest smile, but she wasn't letting him get away with nothing. Not today.

She frowned but he kept smiling.

"No, my dear woman, I couldn't. Now don't be cross. I didn't board the train with these children. I kind of inherited them on my way back here. I was only bringing three out to Clover Springs."

"What they do, multiply?" Aaron joked, causing many around them to laugh.

Wilma sent Aaron a reprimanding glare before taking Father Molloy's arm. "Well, they is here now, so we best get them inside and out of the cold." She looked at the children behind him. Some weren't even wearing coats. "Dear Lord above, could you not have provided them with clothes more suitable to the weather. Some of the little ones look like they are frozen stiff."

"They will warm up, Wilma, with some good food and a little bit of loving care. Miss Carstairs and I have done our best. "

Father Molloy sent her a look that said they would speak later. She took the hint. "Come along children. Let's get you into the nice warm house. I got stew on the stove. I bet you are hungry and thirsty." She kept talking as they filed past her into the house.

CHAPTER 8

Aaron stepped forward just as the blonde-haired girl was about to walk past. Unfortunately, she didn't see him and tripped over his boot. Before he could reach out to catch her, she had fallen face first into the muddy snow slush. The two children who'd been holding her hands thankfully let go at the last second. They looked as if they were going to cry first, but when the girl tried to sit up only to fall again, they burst out laughing.

Once he was assured the girl wasn't injured, Aaron almost bit through his lip in an attempt not to laugh. The girl looked up at him, her eyes flashing.

He swiped his hat off his head at the last minute. "Excuse me, miss, can I help?"

She attempted to stand up again, studiously ignoring his outstretched hand.

"Miss Carstairs, you look funny swimming in the mud," one of the children said. His reward was a glare from the girl, but it only made him laugh even more. Unfortunately, Aaron lost control of himself, too, and started laughing loudly.

"Come on, let me help you up or you are going to be playing in the mud all day."

Without waiting for permission, he lifted her up to her feet. He held her close for a couple of seconds, telling himself it was to make sure she was steady on her feet. He didn't want to let her go. The small bit of exposed skin on her arm was so soft to his touch. And her hair? It had tumbled out of whatever upstyle she was wearing to settle in a cloud of gold around her face.

"Please release me. I think you have done enough already." She hissed, her embarrassment causing her cheeks to flush pink. He made the mistake of looking at her mouth. His brain ceased to function as he wondered what it would be...

"Let me go, you imbecile. Can't you see everyone is staring?" Although she spoke low enough for others not to hear, he couldn't mistake the anger in her tone. He stepped back, remembering his manners.

"I apologize, miss. I didn't mean to trip you up. Welcome to Clover Springs."

The look she threw him suggested exactly what she

thought of her welcome but she didn't say anything more. Instead, she tried to dust the mud off.

"Best let it dry first. It will be easier to brush off then," he offered helpfully.

"Please refrain from addressing me, sir. I think I have benefited enough from our acquaintance for one day. Don't you?" She looked to the boys whose hands she'd been holding. "Come along children. We will soon arrive at our destination."

"Just a few more steps and you will be there. It's that white house on the corner of town."

Aaron couldn't help himself. He knew he annoyed her but still he didn't want to leave her side.

"Is that Hope House?" Her disbelief was evident not only from her tone but from the look in her eyes. She was obviously used to something bigger and grander.

"It is. My brother, Samuel, and his wife, Ellen, help run it with Wilma. She's the lady above talking to Father Molloy.

"Oh, you mean the servant."

Startled, Aaron nearly tripped over his own feet. "No. Wilma ain't no servant. She works in the orphanage. In the school, too, when she has time."

"Really? How extraordinary." The girl looked around her. "Papa told me it would be very different out West but I didn't think standards would be that much lower."

Aaron's blood heated, and not because she was even more beautiful up close. "Beg your pardon, miss."

"In Boston, servants, especially coloreds, don't work as teachers. Well, not teaching white children. They only mix with their own kind and certainly wouldn't be working in a position of authority. Especially in an orphanage for white children."

Servants. Wilma was almost one of the family. Laura certainly saw her that way. As for color? Where did this girl come from, eighteen sixty-two Atlanta? He struggled to keep a handle on his temper.

"Now look here, miss, I am not sure where Father Molloy found you but I guess he can take you straight back. Those opinions are not welcome in this here town no matter how pretty the package they come in."

Aaron stomped off.

* * *

ALICE WATCHED HIM GO. She wasn't sure why he was so upset. She hadn't meant any harm. She was simply repeating what she had been taught. Perhaps he was a servant too. He wasn't well educated that was for certain. His grammar left a lot to be desired. Pity as he had a very attractive smile. She hadn't missed his wide shoulders and muscular toned body. Although his clothes were old and worn, they fit him nicely. When he touched her, her blood had rushed to her head. If he hadn't tripped her up, she wouldn't be covered in mud now. Thankfully she still had her traveling cloak on and it had taken most of the damage.

Forcing her thoughts away from the man, she looked around the town. It wasn't as big as she was expecting. The priest seemed to think he would be able to find homes for all the children here. She wasn't so sure.

She didn't want to think about that now. Tired, stiff and extremely hungry, she hoped there would be somewhere to get something to eat. The woman, Wilma, didn't seem to be expecting them, so a warm meal and hot bath was probably out of the question. Still it could be worse. Bracing herself, she followed her charges into the big white house.

CHAPTER 9

Aaron stomped into the store, swinging the door so hard he nearly hit Katie who was rearranging some Christmas items in the window.

"Who put a burr under your saddle? There's no post yet but even if there was, your letter only went out the other day. It will take time for Mrs. Gantley to find you a bride." Her tone was teasing, although Aaron spotted curiosity in her eyes.

Aaron sighed. *What if his mail order bride turned out to be someone like her?* He scowled. He'd just have to send her back. He couldn't live with someone like that.

"Aaron Higgins, you are going to turn the milk. What's got into you?" Katie prompted as he hadn't answered her first question.

"Father Molloy is back."

Katie's face lit up. "Where is he? Is he following

behind you, I can't wait to see him." She craned her neck as if Father Molloy was standing behind him.

"He's gone straight to Hope House. Wilma is hopping mad. He has a whole string of kids with him at least thirty of them."

"Oh dear. Ellen is going to be rather overwhelmed. She isn't feeling too well either. It being early days and all that. I hope Father Molloy knows what he is doing."

"Ellen don't know the half of it."

Katie's look of surprise meant he had spoken out loud. He didn't mean to.

"Sorry Katie, I met someone outside," he apologized.

"Well, whoever it was sure didn't put you in a good humor. It's not like you to go around frowning. What did they do?"

"Nothing. It's more what they said."

Katie waited expectantly.

He didn't feel right talking about the girl he had just met. Maybe he had misunderstood her.

"Don't mind me. I'm hungry is all. Ma said she left you a list earlier in the week. If it's convenient, I will take it now. I am heading back to the ranch."

Katie called Daniel to help Aaron. "While Daniel gets it together, you might want to drive your wagon closer to the store," she said, her eyes dancing with laughter.

Aaron colored so fast he thought his cheeks would sizzle. How stupid could he look coming into the store for a big order without the wagon? He had left it parked outside Hope House when he visited his brother earlier.

"I will be right back. Wagon is still at Samuel's."

"I will come with you. I can't wait to see Father Molloy and all these children you say he has brought. Sounds like Ellen will need help." Katie took a minute to run upstairs to tell her mother-in–law, who was sitting with Ella and young Danny, where she was going. She came back with a basket of food.

"Must be like the feeding of the loaves and the fishes over there. Every bit helps." She handed Aaron the basket. "What are we waiting for?"

Aaron couldn't answer and his legs wouldn't move. What would happen if the girl said something along the lines of what she had said to him in front of Ellen or Katie? Their tempers were legendary for a reason. He groaned. Just what had he got himself mixed up in?

CHAPTER 10

When they arrived, chaos reigned at Hope House. Wilma had taken one look at Alicia and shown her to the bathroom. Thankfully, they had indoor plumbing. She gave herself a quick wash and changed into the other dress she had in her carpet bag. She wished she had her trunk. She would have been able to dress more appropriately. But then, what would she have worn? Her mother's lessons on decorum hadn't covered what to wear when visiting an orphanage run by an ex-slave in the middle of the Wild West. Alicia sighed deeply wondering if she had made a big mistake coming to Clover Springs. Maybe she should go back to the train station and inquire as to the best route to Leadville. But what about the children? You promised you would help them settle in. You don't know if Leadville will be any better than this town. It could even be worse. Alicia rubbed her hands in her skirts, pushed her hair back out of her eyes and gave herself a good talking to. *You can do this. Walk tall and remember nobody knows anything about you here.*

When she came back into the kitchen, Wilma was busy heating up food. Father Molloy was sitting at the table, his shoulders bent, as if the weight of the world was on them. "Real pity you didn't get here a couple of days sooner, Father, you could have been at Little Beaver's wedding. It was on Thanksgiving." Wilma said looking at the priest, her face showing concern.

She watched a lady called Katie exchange a look with Wilma. The priest didn't seem to register the women were talking to him.

She looked up and her gaze locked on the man who had tripped her in the street. His cheeks turned red before he looked away. *He must be embarrassed.*

"Mr. Aaron, go get Little Beaver and the reverend. I need some help and Father Molloy looks as if he could do with a spiritual adviser," Wilma ordered.

His name was Aaron. It was a nice name. It suited him. She wondered if he lived at the orphanage too with his brother. She watched the look of relief on his face, as he turned to leave the house. Maybe he didn't like being surrounded by so many children.

* * *

AARON WAS RELIEVED to be sent out of the orphanage. He didn't want to stay anywhere near *her,* yet he found himself returning with Little Beaver. The kitchen dissolved into chaos with children racing in the direction of Father Molloy and the blonde girl.

"Whatever is the matter with you all?" Wilma shouted above the shrieks and screams.

"He's an Indian." One of the boys stammered.

"Yes, child, he is. He is also my friend."

"Hardly surprising. The natives must stick together."

Bile rose in Aaron's mouth as the blonde girl's horrible words rang out across the room. The children seemed to go silent just at the moment she spoke so everyone heard her.

Aaron risked a glance at Wilma whose stony expression meant her temper was up. He looked from Ellen to Katie and back. He felt like taking a leap out the window just to escape.

"Now you look here, Miss Carstairs. This here be Clover Springs and in this town everyone is welcome regardless of the color of their skin," Wilma spoke, her hands on her hips.

The girl tossed her head as if to show she had no intention of listening to a negro.

Katie stepped forward but Aaron saw Ellen put a hand on her sister's arm. He held his breath waiting for his sister-in-law to give the visitor the dressing down she deserved.

He watched as Ellen looked the girl up and down, her eyes blazing with anger. "This is not only my town but also my home. Everyone is welcome so long as they keep a civil tongue in their head. If you don't, it won't matter who you think you are, you will find yourself out in the cold. With the weather around here, that won't be a pleasant experience."

"Alicia, please. I asked you to keep your opinions to yourself. Nobody here shares your views," Father Molloy begged.

"Why did you bring her here?" Ellen asked Father Molloy.

"I came to help and to make sure these children go to good Christian homes," the girl protested, although Aaron saw her hands were balled into fists. She's not as tough as she acts.

"These good homes you mention, I guess they don't include the likes of me or Little Beaver?" Wilma wasn't letting the girl get away with anything.

A blush rose on the girl's face but it only served to make her physical appearance even more beautiful.

"White children belong in white homes and white

orphanages." Alicia said coolly, dismissing Wilma with a glance.

"Father..." Ellen's eyes blazed with fury. Aaron didn't fancy the new girl's chances against either of these ladies.

"Alicia Carstairs, that is enough. I warned you to be kind to my friends." Father Molloy turned toward John who was watching the adults, his facial expression a mixture of fear and anger. "John, could you take Miss Alicia upstairs? She would like to lie down as she is feeling under the weather." Father Molloy turned toward Alicia. "John is one of the orphans I mentioned on the train. He lives in Hope House."

Alicia opened her mouth to protest but quickly shut it again. With a disdainful look at all of them she marched after John.

"Where did you find her, Father Molloy?" Ellen asked.

"You should have left her wherever it was." Katie didn't bother to hide her disgust.

Aaron moved toward the door. He hated confrontation but his way out was blocked.

"Katie Sullivan, is that the way you were reared? Never judge a book by its cover, especially in one so young. I suspect Alicia has a very unhappy tale to tell, one totally unsuitable for our young audience." Father

Molloy didn't shout but the group was left in no doubt about his displeasure.

"Maybe, Father, but those hateful views she is spouting are also unfit to be heard by any audience, be they young or old," Katie responded tartly.

"Agreed, Katie, agreed." The priest spoke quietly as if overcome by the enormity of the task he faced. Aaron wished he could do something to help relieve the old man's burden. *If Ma were here, she'd know what to do. You're a grown man not a child. It's time to stop relying on Ma.*

"FATHER MOLLOY, you look very tired. Why don't you go sit in the sitting room? We can feed the children and then the adults can eat. Reverend Tim will be here soon. He will have some ideas on how to help as well." Aaron's tone sounded more confident than he felt but it worked. The priest sent him a grateful look before shuffling off to the sitting room. Wilma beamed at him with approval before rubbing her hands on her apron.

"Right, let's start with the younger ones. Can't feed thirty children at once."

* * *

THEY FED the children in relays. Finally, all thirty-three children had eaten their fill. They were happy to go outside into the back yard to play. Although cold, they were soon running around, obviously glad to be free of the confines of the train. The older boys and girls promised to keep an eye on the younger ones so the adults could eat in relative peace.

Exhausted, Wilma and all the other helpers sat down to eat. Father Molloy didn't join them. Instead, he and Reverend Tim were talking in the sitting room. Wilma had taken a tray into them earlier.

"I saw you speaking to Miss Alicia on the street, Mr. Aaron. Maybe you should go up and knock on her door, tell her it's time to eat," Wilma muttered.

"Not on your life. I ain't going anywhere near that woman," Aaron vowed crossly.

"Leave her be for a while, Wilma. She probably wouldn't welcome our company anyway. I doubt we are what she would consider her equal," Ellen said, her tiredness making her sound weary.

"What is she doing here? For all her act and the way she speaks, you would expect her to be living in a big house in Boston. She reminds me of Mrs. Shipley," Katie said.

"Lawrence's mother? I think those two would get on like a house on fire," Ellen said, her eyes sparkling with temper.

Samuel and Aaron exchanged a look. Aaron almost pitied the young woman. Almost but not quite.

"Wonder what she is doing here with those children. She's a bit young to be left in charge of them all, isn't she?"

Ellen's question put Aaron's thoughts into words. Not that he wanted to admit his mind was still consumed with the girl.

"What age do you think she is?" Samuel asked.

"About nineteen I reckon. Not much older than that." Aaron surprised himself as much as the rest of them by commenting. He caught the speculative gaze Katie threw in his direction.

"I think she be about that, Mr. Aaron. We should all wait to get to know her a little before we go judging her." Wilma sighed. "I was wrong to speak so cruelly to her. She may have had a terrible journey and is tired."

Judging by the silence around the table, Aaron didn't think anyone agreed with Wilma but they weren't brave enough to say so. He certainly didn't. He wished the girl had never come to Clover Springs. *So why can't you get her out of your mind then?*

"Many reasons why people behave as they do. To say something so ugly, usually means you are hiding big hurt. In here." Little Beaver pointed to his chest.

"They should make you a preacher rather than

deputy sheriff," Aaron teased his friend trying to lighten the atmosphere. He loved the people around this table and didn't want anything, or anyone to hurt them. No matter how nice she looked, he told himself firmly.

* * *

ALICIA LAY on top of the bed; in the room the young boy had shown her too. He seemed nice and polite despite his color. Coming here had been a mistake. Not only was she expected to treat Indians and Negros equally, but almost every woman seemed to be Irish. Her father had an even lower opinion of them than he had of natives.

Papa. She was alone for the first time in almost a month so she could let the tears come. *Oh Papa, why did you have to do it?*

She pushed her head into her pillow so the people downstairs wouldn't hear her cry. She wasn't going to show weakness again to anyone.

Her eyes closing, she thought of Sarah. She hadn't thought of her old nanny in years. She'd been a slave on her aunt's plantation in the South. After the war, her aunt had asked her mama to take Sarah in. The woman didn't want to be free as she didn't know how to read or write. Least that is what Alicia had been told. Now she wondered if it had been more lies. Why did Papa have to destroy everything? Not just my future but my past. I don't know what to believe anymore.

CHAPTER 11

Aaron fumed the whole way back to the Sullivan ranch. The door banged behind him startling his ma who was adding wood to the kitchen stove.

"What's got into you Aaron? It's not like you to be moody."

"Father Molloy came back to Clover Springs today," Aaron answered his ma as he stepped further into the kitchen in the Sullivan ranch.

"That's wonderful. Wait till I get Mary and you can tell us both."

Before Aaron could stop her, his ma went looking for Mary. She returned with Mary and Laura both holding their baby girls.

"Is it true, you saw Father Molloy? How is he? Where's he staying? What kept him away?"

"Mary, will you give the man a chance to answer. You can't keep firing questions at him," Laura said, although her face was also lit up with curiosity.

"He's back and he brought thirty orphans with him." Aaron picked up the coffee pot and helped himself to a cup. "You should have seen it, Ma. He walked through Clover Springs with all these kids walking after him."

"Why? Where did he find that many children?" Mary asked looking mystified.

"Never mind where he found them, what's he going to do with them? Hope House isn't big enough to fit all of them. Wilma will need some help feeding them," his ma said crossly.

"I don't know the answers, Ma," Aaron said before dunking a cookie into his coffee. His ma usually told him off for behaving like a kid but tonight the news about Father Molloy had her distracted.

"Mary, why don't we go into town tomorrow? We can see for ourselves what's going on and can bring some food with us. Wilma is bound to need some help," Laura said.

"Are you sure you are up to the trip, Laura? I don't want to land on Mrs. Grey's bad side for wearing you out." Ma looked closely at Laura but she seemed in good health to Aaron. He wished the women would leave so he could speak to his ma in private.

"Stop fussing, Mrs. H. I am fine now, aren't I, darling?" Laura cuddled her baby closer. "It's about time I got to show off Victoria."

"Mrs. H, can you take Cathy? I am going to go find some of those quilts Ma Sullivan made over the years. We have lots of them so we can lend some to Ellen."

"Come here to me, Cathy, I haven't had a cuddle in hours."

Aaron almost stamped his feet in frustration. He'd wanted to speak to his ma but he wasn't going to start talking about women in front of these ladies.

"What ages were the children, Aaron? They can't be all babies."

"No, Miss Laura, there wasn't any younger than two or three but some of the older ones were in their early teens."

"Good maybe there are a couple of older boys who can give Samuel a hand with the chores. Were there any girls to help Ellen?"

Aaron opened his mouth to answer but it had gone dry. He swallowed hard but it was no use.

"Aaron probably didn't notice anyone, Laura. You know what men are like."

"Katie is helping Ellen and Wilma. At least, she was when I left," Aaron said, scratching the back of his neck.

"But Father Molloy couldn't have brought all those

children out alone. He must have some help. Wasn't there any adults with him?"

Aaron's neck heated up so quickly his ma and Laura stopped to look at him.

"Who is putting such a glow on your face?"

"Nobody, Ma."

"Does this nobody have a name?"

"I'm guessing she's pretty," Laura teased.

"She is but only on the outside. She's actually awful," he blurted, barely noticing the shock on the women's faces. "She was horrible to Wilma and Little Beaver. She told Father Molloy white children belong in a white orphanage. You can imagine how her outburst went down." Aaron could have bitten his own lip. What did he have to tell them for? Now they would talk for hours.

"Did Katie slap her? Or Ellen for that matter? They've both become very fond of Wilma," Laura said, anger making her eyes darken.

"Father Molloy sent her for a nap. He must have felt it better to separate everyone."

"There is going to be fireworks in the orphanage if she keeps that up. That settles it. I am going into town tomorrow. Mrs. H you best come with us. Wilma may need calming down. She has no time for white people thinking that way," Laura said, her expression mutinous. Aaron couldn't help feeling sorry for the new girl. *Again.*

"I ain't got time for anyone who thinks like that. She best decide not to make Clover Springs her home and move on quickly. What was Father Molloy doing bringing a woman like that to our happy town?" Ma muttered as she bustled around the kitchen banging pans down on the stove.

Aaron decided it was best to leave her be. He headed to the barn. *Yes, why did Father Molloy have to bring a woman like Alicia? And why couldn't he get her out of his head no matter how upset he was at her words?*

He began mucking out the stalls. He usually hated the task but for now it allowed him to keep busy. His mind was working overtime. Why of all the girls he could have met, could he like one like her? *Maybe because you used to share her views.* The thought hit him sideways. It wasn't quite true. He had nothing against black folk, but weren't his views of Indians something similar until he got friendlier with Little Beaver and Nandita? That was different, they killed your pa. Maybe something bad had happened to Alicia's parents to make her feel so strongly.

Oh heck, there is no point on dwelling on it now. Even if she didn't hold such horrible views, she would be out of his league anyway. It was obvious she came from a wealthy background. Her bearing and accent marked her as such. She wasn't the right woman for a ranch hand. Her type belonged in the big cities where they could dress up and attend the opera or other society occasions.

CHAPTER 12

Alicia woke up, amazed it was morning and she had slept so long. She hadn't even undressed. Her clothes were so wrinkled but it couldn't be helped. She didn't know where her trunk was.

Some of the children from the train were still asleep in her room. She stepped over a couple of them lying on rugs on the ground making her way downstairs. Taking a deep breath, she pushed the door open. Judging by the tantalizing smells, the kitchen wasn't empty.

Wilma, the woman she had met the night before, looked up as she came in. She smiled obviously making an effort to be friendly. Alicia wasn't sure how to respond. Her mama always told her to keep servants at a distance but this woman wasn't her servant.

"Did all the children stay here?" she asked.

"Yes, Miss Alicia, they did. John, he's the boy who showed you to your room last night, and his sister Rosa, they gone to stay with Ellen and Samuel. They live in a house right next door. The other children are all spread out between the six bedrooms upstairs. I slept down here with a couple of the older ones."

"You gave up your room for the children?"

"Yes, of course, they needed the rest. Have you been traveling for long? Father Molloy was really too tired to explain how ye all met last night."

Alicia panicked. She didn't want to explain anything to anyone yet. She tried to change the subject.

"Is there something I can do? I don't know how to cook but I could set the table."

"Could you go check on the little ones please? They know your face and it will be hard for them waking up somewhere new," Wilma said before turning to check something on the stove.

Alicia didn't trust herself to say anything. The woman was being really kind. She didn't treat the children as an inconvenience. Maybe the priest was right. This was the best home for them.

Alicia climbed back up the stairs going into one of the rooms where the younger girls were sleeping.

"That you, Alicia?"

"Yes, Tilly, it's me. Did you sleep well?"

"I love it here. We had lots of food last night and then we played. The Indian man said he was going to take David and some of the other boys out hunting. Do you think he would bring us girls?"

"Absolutely not! The very idea," Alicia said quickly, her sharp tone bringing a tear to the young girl's eyes. "I'm sorry Tilly; I didn't mean to speak so sharply. It isn't seemly for nice girls to go out hunting. That's the men's job."

"Why?" Tilly questioned.

"What do you mean why? That's just the way it is. You will have to help me to get the others dressed. We won't find them new homes if they look like they play in the gutter." Alicia hoped her firm tone would be enough to stop the questions. She didn't want to have to explain to the younger girl that her sex would dictate what actions and future career society felt would be acceptable.

"Is that what we are doing today? Can we not stay together at Hope House a while longer? I like being with you Alicia." Tilly didn't look up, her cheeks turning pink as she spoke about her feelings.

Shocked, Alicia stared at the younger girl. Nobody

had ever wanted to stay with her before. People she thought were friends disappeared after Papa died. Robert did too. Bitterness made her feel ill. She didn't want to think of her fiancé now. To think he had never been interested in her. All he wanted was her father's money and connections. When they were no longer around, neither was he.

She pushed those thoughts to the side. No matter what had happened in the past, it was partly up to her to ensure these children would be happy.

"Come on, Tilly, let's get the rest of the children up. I smelled bacon and pancakes downstairs. I'm hungry, aren't you?"

"Oh yes, Alicia, I'm starving."

Alicia hid a smile as once more her distraction attempt worked. Some of the children were already awake and dressed, others were still fast asleep. They agreed to sit down at breakfast in groups to make it a bit more manageable.

Alicia was helping one of the youngest girls in the group to eat when the door opened admitting a group of women. She hung back wishing she'd had a chance to change her clothes but her trunk was still at the station. They weren't going to think much of her wearing a wrinkled dress with her hair in a simple braid. She ran a hand over her head, pushing the loose strands out of her eyes.

"Oh, Miss Mary and Mrs. H, you are an answer to prayers." Wilma greeted the women with a big warm smile. The smile faded to be replaced by an angry frown when the third lady entered carrying a very young baby. "Miss Laura, what you done coming to town? You should be resting."

"Wilma, darling, take the frown off your face, you will frighten Victoria." The lady called Laura gave Wilma a one handed hug, her other arm holding the baby.

Wilma melted at the sight of the baby. Wiping her hands on her apron, she held them out for the child. "Give me a look at my grandchild. Isn't she so pretty?"

Alicia's mouth hung open. The white baby was Wilma's grandchild. This was a strange town. Before she could hide, the ladies turned their attention to the children eating.

"Good morning, children, we are some of Wilma's friends. We have come to help."

"Morning!" The children chorused back, some of them speaking with mouths full of food. *Oh no, what will they think of me.* To her amazement the ladies only smiled wider as they turned their attention to her. "Nice to meet you too. Are you the young lady who helped Father Molloy?"

"Yes, ma'am." Alicia almost curtsied. "My name is Alicia Carstairs."

“Nice to meet you, Miss Carstairs. My name is Bertha Higgins; I am Samuel's ma. This here is Mrs. Laura Kelley and Mrs. Mary Sullivan. The lady coming in at the back is Mrs. Grey. She came to check the children. Mrs. Grey works with our doctor and his other nurse, Emer.”

Alicia nodded at each of the ladies. They looked very nice but then they didn’t know anything about her. Once they heard her shameful story, they would cross the street rather than speak to her. She wasn’t under any illusions about that.

"Wilma, we brought some things. Mrs. H packed food and I took out some extra blankets and quilts we had in storage. We thought you might need them. Where is Father Molloy?”

"Right behind you, Mary Sullivan."

Alicia watched as the grown woman squealed before throwing herself at Father Molloy. The priest wasn’t offended but seemed to enjoy the attention.

“Father Molloy, why did you leave Clover Springs so suddenly? You missed so much. It couldn’t be because of these children. You said it was luck you met with them.”

“Yes, it wasn’t planned. Not sure luck had anything to do with it. God wanted me to find these children.”

"Well yes, of course, but why did you leave Clover

Springs? We were all so worried about you," Mary repeated.

"There were some issues in Boston that needed my attention."

Alicia looked closely at the priest. He was hiding something. Bad news she guessed by his expression and the reluctance to talk. Wilma must have shared similar thoughts.

"Miss Mary, would you leave the poor man alone. I bet he can't string a sentence together. Can you imagine making that train journey with thirty children? I feel quite faint at the thought." Wilma fanned herself with her apron making everyone laugh.

"Okay, I will stop asking questions," Mary said. "For now."

"Are you planning on staying this time, Father?"

"I don't know, Ellen, and that is the honest truth. I may have to go back to Boston. Only time will tell."

CHAPTER 13

Father Molloy and Reverend Timmons withdrew to another room for a private talk. Wilma and the other ladies made coffee and started sorting through the items Mary had brought with her. Alicia decided it was a good time to leave before they sat down and started asking her difficult questions. She wasn't ready to talk about her past and given she knew little of her future it wouldn't be enough to make conversation. "Excuse me ladies, I will be back later to help with dinner."

Alicia almost ran out of the kitchen to prevent any of them from stopping her. Alicia spotted Samuel walking through the back yard. If she hurried, she'd catch him.

"Mr. Higgins, I don't mean to cause trouble, but is there someone who could collect my trunk from the station? I left it there yesterday to walk the children to Hope House."

"I'll ask Aaron to get it for you. I would go myself but my days of lugging a trunk are over," Samuel answered, his eyes holding her gaze.

Embarrassed she'd been caught staring at his horrific injuries, Alicia looked away. "I'm sorry. I forgot my manners," she apologized softly.

"No need to apologize. I am not as handsome as I used to be, that's for sure."

She stared, amazed he could make so light of his injuries. They looked painful.

"Was your accident recent?" *Why had she asked him that? Ladies didn't ask personal questions.*

"About six months ago now. Hope House, the first one, burned down. I happened to be inside at the time."

"Oh my goodness. You were lucky to escape."

"I wasn't lucky. My brother, Aaron, and my friends, Davy Sullivan and Little Beaver, rescued me. They all risked their lives that night."

The Indian had saved a white man? With everything she had heard about Indians, she found that hard to believe. She stared at Samuel as she processed her thoughts.

"I can see I've upset you. I didn't mean to," he said stiffly as the silence lingered.

"No, not at all," Alicia spoke quickly trying to make up for her silence. "I am very glad you got out. Glad, too, you were able to salvage Hope House. The children wouldn't have anywhere to go if you hadn't."

Samuel looked in the direction of the house. "We weren't able to salvage much but the townsfolk got up a collection. Everyone chipped in as much as they could and the result is what you see. Of course, it helped when Davy Sullivan gave us the land and Lawrence Shipley provided the... Are you okay, Miss Carstairs, you've gone very pale."

Her heart beat so fast, she was sure he could hear it. "I'm fine. Just a little tired. I think maybe I should go back to my room." She picked up her skirt and walked quickly back to the house, having to restrain herself from running.

CHAPTER 14

Aaron carried the wood he had cut into the orphanage kitchen, closely followed by Little Beaver. He guessed his friend was here for the same reason. To see how they could help the new arrivals settle into Clover Springs. He put the wood by the stove before gratefully taking the coffee Wilma handed him.

He wondered why Alicia wasn't sitting at the table with the other women but he didn't say anything. The tension was already palpable. He guessed the women were waiting, rather impatiently, for Father Molloy to finish his private chat with Reverend Timmons. Maybe then they would find out more about the plans for the children.

. . .

JUST AS HE finished his coffee, Reverend Timmons came back into the kitchen followed by Father Molloy. Wilma instructed them to take a seat while she poured more coffee.

"Have a slice of pie. I know how much you like Mrs. H's pies," Wilma teased.

Aaron accepted a slice of pie and a refill of coffee as Katie started questioning the priest.

"So, Father Molloy, what's the plan for these children?"

"I am waiting for God to answer that question Katie. I'm afraid I haven't had a chance to think this one through. The children were in danger. I had to act."

"How come you got so many? Wasn't there anyone else to take them?"

"I didn't bring them from Boston. I met them on the train to Denver. They were being taken to work in the mines in Leadville. I had to intervene after Alicia brought their plight to my attention."

At the mention of Alicia, Aaron asked, "Miss Carstairs wasn't taking the children to work in the mines, was she?"

"No, not at all. Miss Carstairs intervened when one of the children was abused by the person escorting them. She was extremely brave and acted without thought for her own safety."

So she has a good side.

"Why would they want children in the mines? They aren't strong enough to mine coal," Katie asked.

"You'd be surprised. Children have been working down in the pits in England for years now. The seams are quite small and children, being smaller and thinner than most men, fit better. They can do jobs a grown man can't," Father Molloy said sadly.

"I guess the mine owners or their foremen don't care too much about the health of those kids. If they die, there are plenty more to replace them."

Shocked silence greeted Wilma's words. Aaron had to swallow hard to get past the lump in his throat. *He couldn't imagine the children he had seen playing outside could have ended up in such danger.*

"Wilma, your knowledge of human conditioning astounds me every time. I don't know how you know all that you do," Father Molloy spoke, his voice sad and tired.

"That be easy. I came from a place where children were sold like animals. The fact that the ones you got are white is the only difference, ain't it Father?"

"Children aren't sold as slaves. That doesn't happen these days," Aaron protested but Father Molloy disagreed.

"You would think not, but it actually happens more often than we would like. These children weren't slaves as such. They will be paid something for their labor. As I said, the children are smaller and can fit into smaller seams. They are also cheaper to feed and house."

Aaron's stomach turned. He couldn't imagine working so far underground away from the light, the sun.

"What about the younger children?" Ellen asked, her voice quivering.

"I am not completely sure." Father Molloy lifted his coffee cup but put it back down on the table without drinking. "Having met the two people in care of the children, I would assume the worst. I have heard of orphanages with a policy of selling children to rich couples. Some of those children end up in fine homes. Others are sadly abused."

Katie pushed away her coffee. "I feel sick. The landlords treated us badly in Ireland but they didn't steal our children away to be sold."

"These children don't have parents, least not that we know of. Some of them are foundlings, those left at the church steps perhaps because the mothers are unwed. Others are victims of tragic accidents, their parents killed while working or dying from diseases caused by mining and other occupations." Father Molloy twisted his hands together. The old man looked overwhelmed and for the first time since meeting him, Aaron thought he looked every year of his age.

"So what are we going to do with them? Won't the people who think they own them come looking for them?" Aaron asked partly wishing someone would come looking. He would take great pleasure in giving him or them a kick in the backside. *Better keep those thoughts to myself as priests don't tend to agree with revenge.*

"I don't believe so. I think they would prefer to sink back into the background. Unfortunately, there is one thing we are not short of in America and that is poor children," Father Molloy answered.

"Well, I am glad you brought them to Clover Springs. We are going to find homes for each one of those children. It will be Christmas soon. What better Christmas present can you give to a child?" Katie stood up from the table as if she meant to go out today and find a home for every child.

"But, Katie, not everyone will be keen to take in a stranger. You don't know where these children came from." Aaron knew he sounded defeatist in the face of Katie's optimism. He preferred to think he was being realistic.

"Aaron Higgins, you sound like Charlie Staunton. I don't care where these children came from, but they are not going to end up down any mine, never mind worse places. Not while there is a breath in my body."

Aaron had never felt the full force of Katie's temper before. He pitied anyone who stood in her way. "Sorry, Katie. I believe we should help the children. I just meant not everyone will feel the same."

Katie nodded giving him a weak smile, her eyes looking suspiciously watery. He hoped she didn't cry. He wasn't very good around crying women.

"You did the right thing bringing them here. If there is one thing I have learned, it's that when the people of Clover Springs pull together they get things done." Reverend Timmons stood up. "I best be getting back to Mrs. Timmons. I have a feeling once she hears you have children who need homes, my wife might be the first in line."

Little Beaver stood. "I have to get back too. The sheriff's office won't run itself. I will not be able to help with homes for the children but I can help with food. I go hunting and bring back meat. I can teach the older boys how to hunt too."

"The women of this town need to get together and get working. We now have another thirty plus children to make presents for as well."

Katie went to take her shawl from the peg.

"Wilma, I know you are tired but make sure Father

Molloy has a good meal. Father, did you not sleep well at the boarding house?"

"Katie, your mother-in-law always provides a fine comfortable bed. But last night, my mind was going around in circles thinking about these poor children. I am so glad all my friends are willing to help me out. I knew coming here was the right thing to do." Father Molloy paused for a couple of seconds. "May God bless you all for your efforts."

"He better bless me with some patience. With your newest protégée, Miss Carstairs, I think I may need it."

Everyone laughed.

"I best be getting back to the store. Daniel will think I got lost."

"Wait for me, Katie, I will walk with you," Little Beaver said. "Aaron, you coming?"

"No. I will stay here and cut some more wood for the fires. I think the children could do with a bath." Aaron wrinkled his nose making everyone laugh once more.

DESPITE THE LAUGHTER, Wilma caught the look of sadness on the priest's face. "Ellen, why don't you and I gather up those children and get them ready for their baths." The shrieks of the children playing came in from the yard. "Come on, school teacher, you be used to a gaggle of children. Show me how it's done. Aaron get chopping. We'll need to keep the stove hot."

Wilma turned to Father Molloy.

"Father Molloy, you go back to the boarding house and rest. You won't be any good to anyone if you collapse from tiredness. We can talk again tonight after dinner."

Aaron walked out the door after Father Molloy. He had work to do. It was only cutting logs but at least it would help those children. If he was married, would his wife be willing to give a stranger's child a home? *Bit much to expect her to come out here, marry someone she's only met and then land her with a child all at once.* Aaron swung the axe harder.

CHAPTER 15

The day passed in a flurry of activity. Alicia came downstairs when she heard most of the people had gone. Mrs. Grey had gone back to the doctor's office after insisting Laura take Victoria home saying both needed their rest.

Mrs. Higgins and Mary stayed to help with the baths. Alicia worked side by side with the women marveling at how well they all got on with the job in hand.

After every child had been washed and the tubs of dirty water disposed of, Wilma made some lunch and insisted they all sit down to eat.

"Wilma, I think the youngest child was about two years old. Who would send them away?" Ellen wondered aloud, her other hand rubbing her stomach as if protecting the child, she carried.

"The people who sent these children ain't thinking of them as human beings. They is goods to them. A profit margin that's all they be seeing, Miss Ellen." Wilma stirred her coffee for a few minutes. "I wonder how many people in Clover Springs will want to take on children."

Mary nodded. "It's been a hard winter after the drought in the summer. People are hurting financially."

"I wonder if your sister knows how hard a battle she will face." Mrs. Higgins said looking at her daughter-in-law, a fond smile on her face.

Ellen sighed. "If there is anything my sister is good at, it's fighting against the odds. With us to help her, she will find a way."

Alicia stayed silent. From what little she had seen of the town, she didn't think the chances of finding all the children homes was too high. But she wasn't about to say that aloud. She jumped as she heard Aaron's voice in the hallway. He was talking to Samuel.

"Where do you want this, Miss Carstairs?"

"Thank you for getting it," she said, hoping her voice wouldn't squeak. She tried to mimic what she remembered of her mother's tone when dealing with hotel staff. "Please take it to my room."

Aaron's eyebrows rose at her command but he didn't say anything. He simply turned, lifted the trunk as if it was a light piece rather than a heavy case and headed up the stairs. Samuel called directions after him.

Alicia turned to find all the ladies staring at her. "Please excuse me." She stammered, her nerves making her sound like a small child. "I would like to check my things."

She waited for Aaron to come downstairs before rushing to her room. She desperately needed to be alone. She didn't want anyone to see her looking through her trunk. She was bound to end up in tears. Sometime later, she heard Mary and Mrs. Higgins saying goodbye but she didn't come down.

CHAPTER 16

Aaron decided to stay in town that night taking advantage of a spare bed in Samuel's house. He wanted to see what Father Molloy and the others had decided to do about the children. He knew Katie thought they ought to find homes for all of them but that was going to be difficult. He rubbed his shoulders, his muscles screaming at him for spending the whole day chopping wood. But at least the woodpiles were now fully stocked again. Little Beaver had warned them months ago it was going to be a long cold winter. It was better being prepared, especially now that so many children depended on the orphanage.

Mrs. Grey, Reverend Timmons, Emer Shipley and Katie had come back to the orphanage after having dinner in their own homes. The children were all in bed. He guessed Miss Carstairs was upstairs with them. *Probably hiding.*

"I think we all agree the children must not end up in the mines but the question is, how do we prevent it? I know the people of Clover Springs want to help but over thirty children are a lot to find places for." Reverend Timmons looked as helpless as Aaron felt. Clover Springs was a small town and the people weren't well off.

"We have to try, Reverend. We just got to do something. What about if we find homes for the boys as a priority? If the boys have been legally adopted, the men who want them to work in the mines can't take them back," Katie said, her head nodding in her eagerness to find an answer.

"I guess that could be one solution, although girls work down the mines too. What do you think, Mrs. Grey?"

"You won't like what I am about to say, Reverend Tim, but we must be realistic. There are many reasons why the boys would be attractive to the people of Clover Springs. Labor isn't cheap so why not adopt a couple of children and have them work for you for free."

"Our residents wouldn't do that?" Reverend Timmons protested but Aaron didn't think he was fully convinced.

"Wouldn't they?" Mrs. Grey asked, her tone suggesting that some of the residents would be more than willing to adopt boys for this very reason.

"Well, maybe some of them would but we just have to be selective. There is nothing wrong with a child doing chores around his home but we are not in the business of providing child labor." Reverend Timmons sounded more sure of himself.

"Is there any risk the people who paid for these children to travel will come looking for them Father?" Katie asked.

"I don't believe so but obviously, I cannot rule it out completely. My guess would be Alicia is the only one who remains at risk."

Aaron's stomach churned at the priest's remark. *Alicia was in danger.*

"Father, why do you think Alicia is in more danger than the children?" Ellen asked, her face white. "I didn't think she was traveling with them."

"She wasn't. It is only by the Grace of God, I met her on the train. Her bravery saved the children and led her here. She believed she had secured a job as governess with a family by the name of Oaks."

"You have reason to believe otherwise?" Aaron couldn't believe his voice sounded so normal when his pulse was racing.

"Unfortunately, yes I do, Aaron." The priest took a

deep breath. "It has to do with why I rushed back to Boston. It seems there is a group of men like Coleman and Johnny who are preying on vulnerable young women."

"Nothing good came of anyone who reminds you of those two." Wilma's eyes sparkled with anger.

"Well, instead of offering the girls a job in their saloons, they lure them to Leadville and other mining towns on the pretense of offering respectable employment."

"You mean there was no governess job with the Oaks family?" Ellen asked quietly.

"Unless Mr. Oaks has the need for numerous governesses. I am afraid not." Father Molloy lapsed into silence.

"How did you find out about it?" Ellen asked, half of her not wanting to know the answer.

"One of the girls escaped. She wrote to a friend of mine. I cannot tell you who as the girl in question is terrified she will be found. Anyway, she told my friend the story behind this ring. The girls are collected at the station, taken to what they believe is their employer's residence, compromised and then forced into the only life available."

"Oh the poor girls. Why has something not been done about this?" Ellen's eyes were full of tears.

"Money talks, Miss Ellen," Wilma said.

Father Molloy nodded his agreement. "Usually, the girls come from orphanages. It seems the gentlemen behind the ring have been very generous in their donations to several orphanages. As you know money breaks down barriers faster than most anything else. They are seen to be good citizens and so the girls are entrusted into their care. Orphanages rarely enquire as to the health and happiness of former residents as we well know."

Aaron's horrified tone rang out in the silence following Father Molloy's words.

"Why would a cultured well brought up young lady fall victim to that type of scam?"

"It appears her father died recently and she was left to her own devices. I am not surprised. There are few opportunities for well brought up young ladies. These men know what they are doing."

Aaron clenched his fists under the table. He burned with anger at the men who could treat innocent young women like that. But mostly he was annoyed at the effect Miss Carstairs had on him. At first, he was attracted to her looks, but after hearing how she had stood up for the children on the train, he found himself wanting to protect her. *How could you want to hold sometime tight and never let them go while at the same time hate the views they held?*

"To think Alicia could have ended up in a place like

that. I know she has upset us all with her views but she is a product of her upbringing. Nobody deserves a life like the one you described."

Everyone nodded at Mrs. Grey's comment. All except Aaron, he was still too angry. "We can't let her travel to Leadville. Not now we know what could happen. What are we going to do?"

Father Molloy looked straight at Aaron. "I don't know. I fear the situation has become rather dangerous. I was coming back to Clover Springs to discuss the situation with Laura and Wilma. Given their backgrounds and knowledge of men like Johnny and Coleman, I thought they may be able to give me some advice as to how to proceed. There is little point in arresting the Mr. Oaks of this world. We need to find the ringleaders and get them jailed."

"The information we have is very old and probably out of date. Sure, we could give you the names of places Johnny liked to visit. Where his friends, men just like him, would go for an afternoon or evening entertainment. I am not sure how much use it will be," Wilma said.

"So does this mean you will be leaving again, Father?"

"I don't know the answer to that, Ellen. My inquiries have upset quite a few people. I was warned it may be prudent to keep my head down for a while."

"You need to rest. You have aged terribly since you left."

"Thank you very much, Katie."

Katie held her hands over her heart. "Sorry Father, I have to stop saying exactly what I am thinking. Us Irish are far too direct."

"I don't mind. I know your heart is in the right place, Katie. I confess I am feeling rather tired lately. I may just stay in Clover Springs for a while. It would be nice not to have to watch my back all that time."

"And you get to eat well too. Between Ma Sullivan and Mrs. H you will be spoiled."

"Have you told Miss Alicia the truth about her offer of employment?"

"Not yet, Wilma. I was hoping she might decide to stay in Clover Springs of her own accord. But given her views, she may feel she needs to live elsewhere. I found out she does have some family on her mother's side. Perhaps she could go live with them."

"You got to tell the sheriff what you know. There must be US marshals involved already if these men have been doing this for some time. We need to get proper help." Aaron colored. "No offense, Father."

"None taken. I agree entirely."

* * *

ALICIA STOOD SHOCKED to the core. She knew listening at the door was the height of bad manners but she hadn't meant to. She had come looking for a glass of water for one of the children. Just as she was about to open the door, she overheard Father Molloy talking about her and Mr. Oaks. The reality hit her. She had been conned into thinking she was going to be a governess. She wasn't completely sure what fate awaited her in Leadville but it certainly wasn't a pretty one. Heart hammering, she turned to walk back up the stairs. Thank God she had followed her intuition and trusted the priest. That's why he had looked funny when she told him the name of her would be employer. He'd recognized it but obviously felt he couldn't share the details with her. Was it because of her views? Did he believe she deserved to go to Leadville? *No, silly. He saved you by bringing you here. He looked out for you. More than anyone else ever has.*

CHAPTER 17

Aaron knew he was staring at Alicia but he couldn't help it. After hearing how close she came to disaster, he wanted to wrap his arms around her and protect her. She touched him in a way no other woman had. He yearned to reach out to touch her hair to see if it was as soft as it looked. She was looking at him, her eyes clouded with doubt, as if waiting for his answer. She must have said something.

"Sorry what did you say?"

"I asked you if the children were okay in school. I was worried someone might pick on them. You said you had just checked with Ellen to see if she had sufficient wood for the stove. It being so cold and all."

She was talking too fast not to be unnerved by his presence. He wondered what had her so anxious. He sought to reassure her.

"The children will be fine. Ellen won't let anything happen to them."

"Oh, I didn't mean to imply she would."

He took a step toward her, his hands raised as if in surrender.

"Stop. Miss Carstairs, we always seem to end up with a misunderstanding. I know you didn't mean anything. I was just saying the children will be fine." Deciding he needed to turn on the charm, he tried flattery. Ma said all women liked to be told they looked good. "What are you going to do with your time today? You look very smart in your outfit."

"This old thing?" Alicia looked down at her dress.

He was no fashion expert but her clothes looked barely worn. They fit her beautifully. He guessed she didn't buy them from a store. Yet another example of how different their backgrounds were.

Aaron knew he should go and get some work done but he couldn't drag himself away from Miss Carstairs. He wanted to spend the whole day with her. To find out what made her laugh, why she looked so anxious. How she came to be on the train. Everything.

"Mr. Higgins?"

"Sorry, yes, Miss Carstairs?"

"I just asked you whether you were waiting to see Samuel. He went out earlier and I am not sure when he will be back."

"No. I got to go. I have to go to the store for Ma. Have a good day, Miss Carstairs."

Great, now you look like a complete country bumpkin. I bet the city men are much better at making conversation.

* * *

ALICIA STARED AFTER HIM. What was it about the man she found so attractive? Was it the fact he seemed more real than the men she was used to mixing with in Boston? He smelled of the outdoors, with a strong hint of horse. He wasn't handsome but he had a kind face and eyes that seemed to stare right into her soul. She knew it wasn't proper for him to touch her, yet the slightest touch of his fingers sent shivers through her entire body. She found herself watching for him all day wondering if he would call to see his brother. They seemed like a close family but given Wilma's teasing, she got the impression Aaron called into the orphanage more now than before. Or was that wishful thinking on her part? He couldn't be coming to see her. He had made his feelings about her quite plain that first day when she had made those comments. Biting her lip, she wondered if she had kept her opinions to herself, would he have been more open about his intentions. *What intentions?*

CHAPTER 18

Alicia walked through the town. She had agreed to help Ellen at the school. It seemed only right to repay some of the kindness she had received since coming to the town. As she looked around, she could hardly believe a small community like this one had turned everything she believed on its head. Her father had been the center of her world and she'd believed everything he'd told her. She couldn't believe she'd accepted his judgements of other races and cultures as gospel. So far, she hadn't seen any of the Irish ladies drink. In fact, there had been no mention of alcohol at all. They seemed to behave just like the other women she knew in Boston. Well, that wasn't true. The women here were kinder and their friendships seemed deeper. Her mother had plenty of friends and was forever going to social occasions but she didn't remember her mother being as comfortable around the other society ladies as Katie, Mary and Laura seemed to be.

But her mother had been a cold-hearted woman. She couldn't remember her smiling or laughing. Their relationship had been difficult. It was hard growing up with the most perfect woman as a parent. Her mother hadn't been slow about telling her when she failed to make a good impression which had been often.

She was so engrossed in her thoughts she almost walked into Emer and Lawrence Shipley. Clamping down the urge to run away, she gritted her teeth and smiled.

"Miss Carstairs, how lovely you look today. Lawrence, darling, this is Miss Carstairs. She helped Father Molloy rescue the orphans."

Lawrence Shipley stared at her for a couple of seconds longer than what would be considered polite. Her cheeks flushed as she waited for his condemnation.

"Carstairs? Are you related to William Carstairs?"

Alicia squeezed her eyes shut a couple of times trying to get rid of the black spots. She wasn't going to pass out. It was him. It was the same Lawrence Shipley she had met years ago in Boston. Obviously, he didn't recognize her. But she'd changed a lot in the last few years. Had he heard of her father's death and the circumstances behind it? Surely not. Boston was miles away and according to gossip he wasn't in close contact with his family. Briefly she considered lying but it was against her nature.

"Yes. He was my father."

"I am very sorry for your loss. I met him a few times. Your mother was a beauty." Lawrence tipped his hat at her.

"Yes, she was." He knew, yet he was still talking to her. Maybe he had only heard of the death and not the rest of the gruesome details.

"I thought you reminded me of someone. So what brings you to Clover Springs?"

Alicia stared at him. Was he being kind or had he not heard of what happened to her father.

"Lawrence, stop asking so many questions. Miss Carstairs will be on the next train out of Clover Springs."

Alicia smiled at the lady who'd come to her rescue.

"You must come to dinner one evening, Miss Carstairs. My husband misses talking about Boston. I'm afraid Clover Springs doesn't offer much by the way of entertainment."

"Thank you, Mrs. Shipley. Please excuse me. I offered to help Ellen, I mean Mrs. Higgins at the school and I am already late."

Alicia left as quickly as possible. Mrs. Shipley

looked very kind but the last thing she wanted was to sit down and discuss Boston. She couldn't bear it if her family skeletons followed her here.

* * *

As she got nearer the school, she saw some children fighting in the street. Horrified, she saw Steven being pushed to the ground. Alicia picked up her skirts and ran toward the school yard, not caring who would see her.

"What do you think you are doing?" she shouted at the boy who appeared to be the ringleader. He ignored her and continued, with some other boys, to push Steven.

"Stop it now. Stop it at once." Alicia grabbed Bertram but at the same time he pushed back, making her slip on the snow and fall, sprawled, into the melting slush. She shrieked as she tried to get back up but the mud seemed to suck her down.

A strong hand pulled her out, setting her gently on her feet. "You all right now."

Alicia followed the brown arm up to the face with the big brown eyes. They looked kind but there was a wariness there too. As if he knew she may react badly. She forced herself to be polite. He had acted as a gentleman.

"Thank you. I'm afraid I didn't see the mud; I was too busy trying to stop the boys hurting Steven."

"Let me deal with this. Please?" he said, his voice firm yet kind.

She stood back and watched as he addressed the boys. "As deputy sheriff of this town, I will know why you are fighting?"

"He started it. He called me fat and stupid," Bertram Shaw spoke loudly. "Didn't he boys?" The two children with him nodded their heads vigorously.

"Is this what happened?" Little Beaver asked Steven who stayed silent. "Speak boy, tell me your side of the story."

"He can't," Alicia said, wondering where Harry was. He didn't usually stray far from his younger brother's side.

"Yeah, he's stupid. He can't say a word." Bertram and the other children laughed, Steven's face fell to his chest. Alicia reacted quickly.

"What a horrible boy you are. Do you always make fun of people this way? Steven is not stupid. Something awful must have happened as he wasn't born this way. He can hear. Maybe in time he will speak." Alicia took a deep breath before she continued but Little Beaver got there first.

"If Steven cannot speak, how did he call you fat and stupid?" Little Beaver's question made the smiles disappear from the children's faces. They didn't look so happy now. Alicia waited to see what happened.

"Little Beaver, the new boy didn't do nothing. Bertram and his friends have been picking on the new kids all day. Miss Ellen, she told him off a few times. Even sent him to the corner but he hasn't stopped." John came running over, Harry following in his wake. Harry went to stand by Steven, putting his arm protectively around the little boy's shoulders. Alicia wanted to hug him but knew he would reject her. He still hadn't forgiven her for what she had said on the train.

"Thank you, John. Where is Miss Ellen now?" Little Beaver asked.

"One of the girls fell and hurt her arm. Miss Ellen is in the school room with Mrs. Grey."

"Children, listen to me. If anyone makes trouble for the new children, I will take them to the jail house. Now go on home before Miss Ellen comes out and gets really mad."

They turned to go.

"Bertram, wait."

The boy stood, a sulky expression on his face.

"You must apologize to Steven and to his friend Miss Alicia."

"Sorry."

"You must say it as if you mean it."

The boy repeated his apology his tone less surly. "Harry, you go on back to the orphanage with Steven and the others. Bertram, you will go find your mother and tell her she will need to replace Miss Alicia's dress."

"Oh, that's not necessary."

"You hear the lady, she said I didn't have to."

"I am the law in this town. You do have to. Miss Alicia is only being nice. Now go on."

Bertram walked away slowly, his shoulders almost meeting his knees.

"Thank you, emm..."

"Little Beaver is my name."

She flushed wondering just how many times he would have to tell her his name before she could remember it. He must think her very rude.

"You are welcome. The children will be fine but you can expect these type of fights for a few days. It is always the same. Even animals will give the new arrival in the nest an uncomfortable time for a while."

With that he was gone leaving Alicia staring after him. What a strange but nice man. She smiled slightly. Her mama would have swooned if she knew her only daughter stood in the middle of a school yard covered in mud from head to toe conversing with an Indian.

"What did you do? Take a mud bath?"

Alicia whirled around to see Aaron atop his horse. He was laughing at her.

"I fell through no fault of my own. You, sir, are no gentleman to be laughing at a lady in distress."

"You didn't seem distressed. You were smiling at me as I rode over."

"Sir, you are mistaken. I wasn't smiling and certainly not looking at you. Good day."

With as much dignity as she could muster, Alicia made her way toward the orphanage, the mud squelching with every step she took. She knew people were looking at her but she held her head high pretending she was walking through the center of Boston in the latest fashions.

On reaching the orphanage, Wilma came running out. She'd obviously spotted her from the window.

"Why, Miss Alicia, whatever happened to you? Are you hurt?"

"Only my dignity. Steven was being picked on and I tried to intervene and fell over."

"Come inside child, you are going to catch your death standing out here in the cold.

"I can't come inside. I will ruin the floors with all this mud."

"Well, you can't get dressed out here. Come on in now. You must have a bath. Samuel, can you ask John and some of the older boys to get the metal bath down for me please. Miss Alicia, well, she fell and now we need lots of hot water."

Embarrassed beyond belief Alicia stood as the mud ran off her. "Here, miss, wrap this around you. We will soon get you clean and dry."

The tears made a stream through the cake of mud on her face. Everyone was being so kind.

"I found some clothes on your bed. If you want anything ironed just let me know." Wilma stood holding out some clean clothes.

"Thank you, Wilma. For this and for being so nice to me."

"One good turn deserves another. John told us the whole story, but he left out the bit about you falling in the mud. He has become quite a fan of yours, young John. That Bertram Shaw is a menace. Now you take your time. Dinner will be waiting for you when you feel ready to come downstairs."

THE WARM WATER felt wonderful as she eased her tired and sore body into the bath. The scent of roses made her think of her mother. Mama's favorite perfume smelled like a garden of flowers in full bloom. What would her mama make of Clover Springs? She wouldn't have stayed around long enough to spend time with any of the people living around here. They wouldn't have been deemed fit and proper society. Yet these same people had provided her with a home and offered more besides food and shelter. They had offered her genuine friendship, something she had never experienced before. But when Lawrence Shipley *tells them my story, they will send me packing.* Her heart beat rapidly as she tried to convince herself they wouldn't care. Maybe they wouldn't blame her. She lay back in the water, trying to calm her thoughts.

As she relaxed in the water, she heard laughter from the rooms below. Aaron Higgins was downstairs. He had a lovely laugh. He was so different from Robert, her ex fiancé. Robert had seemed like a perfect gentleman, he'd always dressed the part, and he'd been invited to the best parties. He had a career not a job. He came from a long line of Boston bankers, although none as successful as the Shipley's or similar families.

Aaron didn't pretend to be a gentleman yet he had proved to be more honorable than Robert. He wasn't as good looking, his hands were hard and calloused, his clothes showing signs of wear, yet when he looked at her, her skin shivered in a way that had never happened with Robert. She had never been as annoyed with Robert as she got with Aaron. He infuriated her, especially when he seemed to make fun of her, but she found she looked forward to it more and more. Was it because his eyes always told her he was teasing rather than being spiteful?

With a dramatic sigh, she plunged her head under the water. Thinking of Aaron Higgins wasn't going to sort out the rest of her life. She had to decide on what she would do after Christmas and daydreaming wasn't going to achieve anything.

CHAPTER 19

The children were back in school leaving the orphanage very quiet. Alicia had cleaned their bedrooms, tried to help with the laundry and was wondering how to fill the time when there was a knock on the door.

"Morning, Wilma, I am not staying. I must get back home. I wondered, Miss Carstairs, if you were free tomorrow? Wilma and some of the ladies are coming to a sewing circle at my house. Normally we would work on another quilt for the orphanage or someone who was in need but tomorrow we have some Christmas gifts to finish. We want to discuss ideas on how to find the orphans a new home. Father Molloy is coming too; he wants to see Mrs. Higgins."

"I would love to if you don't think I will be intruding."

"Not at all. The more the merrier."

"Thank you, Mrs. Sullivan."

"Call me Mary, please."

Alicia watched as Mary said goodbye to Wilma before walking down the street. She waved at some people as she walked. She had a lovely smile. She didn't realize she was staring until Wilma coughed.

"You feeling alright, Miss Alicia?"

"Yes, thank you, Wilma. I was just thinking Mrs. Sullivan, I mean Mary, has a wonderful smile."

'She sure does. She has a heart of gold. You have a nice smile, too, although you don't show it too often." Wilma was smiling so Alicia couldn't take offense.

"Why are you so nice to me, Wilma? I was extremely unpleasant to you when I first came here yet you have never been anything but kind."

"I seen you with the children. I knew you had a good heart even if your mouth say wicked things."

Alicia didn't know what to say so stayed silent.

"I been around a long time, Miss Alicia. Seen a lot of things, good and bad. If you ever need someone to talk to, you come find me. I is a good listener and I won't tell another soul unless you want me too."

"Thank you, Wilma," Alicia managed to croak out.

The next day, Alicia dressed carefully. Her stomach was turning over with excitement, not about the sewing, which she hated, but at the chance to sit and chat with other adults. She wanted to get to know these ladies better. Maybe she could find out why Father Molloy thought the town was so special.

"Christmas is a very special occasion in Ireland, more so than America as we don't have Thanksgiving. Preparations start early as there are so many things to do. Advent, which is what we call the four weeks before Christmas, was a busy time. The outside of every house and building had to be newly white-washed. So, you could say our Christmas started with a bucket of whitewash in the man's hand," Mary said as she sewed.

"Glad I don't live in Ireland. It sounds like a lot of work." Davy grinned at his wife as he swiped a sugar cookie.

"You couldn't not whitewash the house. You would be the talk of the neighborhood. The men did the painting while the women scrubbed the inside from top to bottom. God help you if you didn't do this chore properly. Mam was a lovely woman but she had a strong right hand."

"Did you decorate the house like we do?" Alicia asked fascinated by the different customs.

"We did with holly. It grows everywhere in Ireland. Mam would make it into a wreath to hang on the door. We had to find the piece with the reddest berries as they bring good luck in the new year. We didn't have decorations like you do here. Nobody around us would have paper to waste by cutting it into pretty things for a tree or the walls." Mary took a deep breath. "The landlord was different. The children used to go climbing trees around the big house to see if we could spy his Christmas tree. I'll never forget the first time I saw it for real. The cook smuggled us in one day to see the tree. It was amazing."

"Did the landlord not want you in his house? On the plantations, it was custom for the owner to give out gifts at Christmas," Wilma said, her face a dark mask.

"Some landlords were nicer than others. Ours wasn't keen on the locals." A look of sorrow washed over Mary's face. Alicia was sorry she had asked. She struggled to think of something to say to distract her.

"How do you celebrate the actual day?"

"We would go to Midnight Mass. Everyone fasts until the mass even the young children. You can hear the people's stomachs growling as they pray the priest's sermon won't last too long."

"Mary Sullivan, it's not a heathen your father reared. Take no notice of her, Alicia. Most faithful Catholics have patience and fortitude to listen to their kindly priest." Father Molloy winked at Alicia showing he was teasing Mary.

"Preparations for Christmas start months before.

My mother used to make her Christmas puddings in the summer. Then she would add whiskey to it every couple of weeks to make sure the fruit was well soaked. There is nothing worse than dry pudding."

"You would eat this for dinner?" Alicia thought a fruit pudding was an odd thing to eat as a main meal. Not that she was surprised by the addition of alcohol. Her father had always said the Irish used to drown in Whiskey.

"No silly. It was our traditional dessert. If we could afford it, we would have roast goose for our dinner." Mary sighed. "I can still remember the smells when Mam was cooking. She used to stuff the goose with her own mixture of herbs and onions. I could smell it as we walked back over the fields after mass. Every house had a lit candle in the window. This was to welcome the baby Jesus but was also a sign that strangers were welcome to share in the family's food."

"But if people were poor, could they afford to share?" Alicia asked. Papa had said the Irish were a nation of drinkers and fighters yet this was not the picture Mary was painting.

"It didn't matter. You always made guests welcome at Christmas. Every year, one of us would have the job of putting baby Jesus in the crib. In some houses, it was a special job given to the youngest but in our house Cathy and I always fought over whose turn it was. Mam used to get very cross." Mary rubbed her eyes as if she was about to cry. Wilma rubbed her shoulder before turning to Alicia.

"Paul Kelley, he's Laura's husband, has made us some cribs. You should see his work. A finer nativity set you never did see."

"Did he give one to the orphanage yet? The children will be so excited between that and all the gifts they will be getting."

"So long as they don't forget the true meaning of Christmas," Father Molloy added.

"Ellen won't allow that, Father," Mary retorted before turning her attention to Alicia. "How did you celebrate Christmas, Alicia?'

Alicia took a deep breath hoping she would make her family Christmas sound as idyllic as Mary had described. "Mother loved Christmas. She insisted the servants brought home the biggest tree they could find. She would spend days decorating it with colored balls and other ornaments that a store she favored imported from Germany. She sent Christmas cards to all her friends too. On the actual day, she gave gifts to the servants. They were always practical such as a new scarf or gloves for our driver and a new apron for the cook. One year, she gave the housemaids some material so they could make new uniforms. She got rather upset by what she thought was their lack of gratitude.

Papa sent me down later with some chocolate and fruit for them. They preferred his presents."

"It sounds delightful."

"I suppose but it was very lonely. Papa would have his clients come for dinner. Mother loved to show off her latest dresses from Paris. When I was younger, I had dinner with the servants. I had so much fun. But as I grew into a young lady, Mother insisted I attend the dinner parties. They weren't a lot of fun. At least not until I met…" Horrified, Alicia stopped talking. She couldn't believe she had almost told them about Robert. She wiped her eye hoping they would think she was upset at the memories. "I'm sorry, I still find it hard to speak about my parents."

"Of course you do. When we first lost Mam and Daddy it was horrible. But over time, the pain doesn't go away as much as you learn to live with it. The same will happen with you." Mary smiled before turning her attention back to the scarf she was knitting.

"Has Aaron heard from Mrs. Gantley yet? Wilma, has Ellen said anything?"

Why was Aaron writing to a woman? Alicia stuck the needle in her finger, again. She hated sewing but it wasn't as bad as knitting, and she had to do her bit to make the children's Christmas presents.

"Mrs. Gantley is the bride lady in Boston. She's the one who sent Katie out here to Clover Springs some years back," Wilma explained as if reading Alicia's mind. "Aaron wrote to her to find a mail order bride."

Alicia tried to hold her hand still but inside she was trembling. He wanted to get married. *To a stranger.*

"Funny you ask, Miss Mary. Katie was just saying a couple of days back that Aaron seemed to have lost interest. The first few days after posting the letter to Mrs. Gantley, he was in the store every day wondering about the post. But now, he ain't be in for a week or more."

"Maybe he's been distracted." Mrs. Grey murmured. Alicia felt her cheeks glowing, although she thought she was the only one who heard the remark. She risked glancing at Mrs. Grey. Her amused expression told her she had noticed Alicia's reaction. Embarrassed she tried to focus on her sewing.

How did Mrs. Grey know she was developing feelings for Aaron?

Nobody else knew, did they? She would be mortified if they were laughing at her behind her back. *They aren't like that here.*

CHAPTER 20

"Do you like to ride, Miss Alicia?" Wilma asked her over breakfast a couple of days later.

"I love to. Papa kept horses. I miss it," Alicia answered honestly. She'd been finding it hard to sleep, her thoughts concentrating on Aaron and his mail order bride rather than her own future.

"I am happy to lend you a horse if you wish to accompany the children on a ride. Aaron needs Little Beaver's help out at his homestead so he is taking some of the older children along too," Samuel said before shoveling some pancakes into his mouth. Wilma grumbled at his table manners but he just smiled widely at her and waggled his eyebrows making everyone laugh.

"Thank you. I would love to. Wilma, are you

certain you don’t need me to stay and help with the other children?"

“You go get some color in your cheeks, Miss Alicia. The other children will be just fine.” Wilma put the water on to boil. “I’ll make you some coffee to take with you. There’s a chill in the wind.”

Excited, she ran up the stairs to get ready. Being outdoors was just the thing to take her mind off the conversation she had overheard last night. She returned shortly, dressed in her riding gear, and followed the sound of the children outside as they got ready to go riding. Little Beaver stared but the children laughed.

"What's wrong? Is my hat on sideways?" She asked as they continued to laugh.

"We don't ride side saddle here." Aaron's voice made her skin shiver. What was he doing here?

"Pardon?"

"The ladies of Clover Springs gave up riding side saddle years ago. They wear riding skirts now. Ellen can lend you something. You seem about the same size.” He winked at her before whispering “Don't worry, Miss Carstairs, your dignity will be intact.”

"You, sir, have no manners," she said icily.

Alicia turned and whirled back into the house. How dare he! Oh, he drove her mad.

"Alicia, wait. I can lend you some clothes.” Ellen

came in behind her. "Aaron is right, we are a similar size, although he shouldn't have commented on it quite so loudly. Don't mind my brother-in-law. He isn't used to being around women. Spends far too long in the bunkhouse with the rest of the men. He is always playing jokes on them. He doesn't mean it."

Oh, yes, he does. But she didn't voice her thoughts. Ellen was trying to be friendly, and if she had a different skirt, she could get out of the house and go riding. *You have never ridden astride before. No time like the present. It can't be that difficult.*

Looking in the mirror, she admired how Ellen's skirt looked. It was also much easier to walk in than her usual outfits. *Mama, if you could see me now.* Mama wasn't here and people were waiting for her outside.

She walked back to the group, her head high. "You look real pretty now, Alicia," Tilly called out.

Little Beaver walked over with a horse. "He is gentle and will not give you trouble."

"I am an accomplished rider Mr. Beaver."

"Little Beaver. Yes, but riding like a man is new to you. If you fall off it will hurt."

Alicia blushed but she couldn't say anything. He was right. It would hurt and not only her pride. She let him help her mount. "Thank you, Little Beaver."

Little Beaver nodded before standing back. Alicia prayed she wouldn't fall off but the Indian was right.

The horse was gentle and didn't seem to notice she was new to this style of riding. After the first few minutes, she soon got used to it. She liked it. It was far more comfortable than riding side saddle. She yearned to race off across the countryside but that would be foolhardy.

Little Beaver rode bareback. He was an excellent rider, totally in command of his horse while at the same time able to help the children.

"Beautiful day. It will help them forget their troubles for a while, don't you think?"

Aaron's voice had the same effect as before. She held the reins tighter in case he saw her shiver. *Maybe he would think it was the cold. Probably not. He is so confident; he possibly believes all women will fall at his feet.*

"Why are you frowning? Do you miss your side saddle?"

"Not at all."

"So why the sad face?"

"There is nothing wrong with the horse. It's the company I wish to change."

She expected him to ride off, but instead he burst out laughing. She bristled. What did she have to do to get rid of this man? She froze as he moved closer, leaning in until his lips almost, but not quite, brushed her ear.

"It's a lovely day for a run don't you think?"

Before Alicia got her wits together, he slapped the back of her horse. The poor animal got a shock and set off racing into the distance. She heard someone shouting behind her but she didn't care. Now that the horse was running, she didn't want it to stop. She pushed her heels into his back and egged him on. This was what real freedom tasted like and she loved it.

* * *

AARON WATCHED HER RACE OFF, a big smile on his face. He'd been right. She was an accomplished horse-woman. He urged his horse to move faster until he caught up with Little Beaver and the children.

"What you doing?"

His smile vanished at the look in Little Beaver's eyes.

"If you were a child, I would expect you to act like a fool. She could be hurt."

Aaron knew Little Beaver was right. He had behaved badly. He knew better than to take risks around horses. Alicia could have been thrown, badly injured, or even killed.

"You like this woman. It has your head all messed up. You need to fix it." Little Beaver didn't give him a chance to say anything. Instead, he rode after Alicia leaving Aaron with the children.

Like her? No I don't. Then why am I hanging around the orphanage? I should be working on the homestead. Not sitting here admiring a strange woman who looks very good on horseback.

Alicia remained aloof even when they reached the homestead. He glanced at her a few times trying to read her expression. What did she think of his home? But her face was closed, like a mask. Little Beaver was still angry. He answered Aaron's questions with single syllables. Finally, he asked Alicia to race him and they both set off. Aaron and the children were left watching.

Frustrated with himself, he told the children to head back in the direction of town. "Please let us stay out a while longer? It hasn't been very long," the children whined.

"The weather is getting worse. We should head back just in case it starts to snow."

He saw a couple of them glance at him in disbelief but one look at his face was enough for them to turn back toward town.

* * *

ALICIA LOVED the feel of the wind in her hair as she raced Little Beaver. She knew he was allowing her to win but she didn't care. She was free. Being out here was so peaceful. She had been pleasantly surprised at Aaron's homestead. It was basic but the location was incredible. The mountains at the back rose almost into the sky. The creek was frozen in places but she could imagine how pretty it would be in the summertime. If she lived out here she wouldn't have to worry about what people thought of her background.

All too soon, Little Beaver had caught up with her. "Miss Alicia, you must turn back now. The weather is changing and it is not good for us to get caught in a snow storm. We have traveled too far already."

Remorse gripped her. "I'm sorry Little Beaver, I got carried away."

"It made you happy, no?" Little Beaver's eyes twinkled as he smiled at her.

"Yes, it did."

"It was worth it then. Being happy will help melt the sadness in your heart."

Before she could answer, he had turned and was cantering back toward town. She duly followed suit, not wishing to dwell on how right he was.

Just as they got to the edge of town, Alicia coughed hoping to attract Little Beaver's attention.

"I am very sorry for how I treated you when we first met. You have been very kind."

"No sorry needed. You see things with your eyes now, not someone else's."

It took her a couple of seconds to understand but when she did, she grinned. He smiled back.

"If you would like to go riding again, you tell me and I will go with you. Please do not go out alone. The weather can change very quickly. It can be dangerous."

"Thank you, Little Beaver. I would love to."

CHAPTER 21

Reverend Timmons and Father Molloy celebrated a joint service at the church. They told the townspeople about the orphans' plight and asked those who might like to find room in their home for another child to stay behind after the service.

"Katie, did you see how many people looked interested? Maybe finding homes for the children isn't going to be as difficult as we first thought." Ellen said as she juggled her niece, Ella, on her knee. Katie was busy with Danny and the little girl didn't like to sit through service. She said it was too boring.

"I don't think there are enough people here to make a real difference," Katie said soberly, reducing Ellen's optimism.

"Stop looking on the dark side. Mam always said

hope didn't have a price. We just have to pray people listened to Father Molloy and realize how special these children are."

Ellen looked around the church dismayed to find not everyone was waiting behind.

"I guess you are right, Ellen. Those people who are running home are probably afraid of the weather. Mary didn't come to church today and she wouldn't miss it unless Davy thought it wasn't safe to travel."

Katie sighed. Ellen gave her sister's hand a squeeze. Her sister thought she could help everyone but the reality was they couldn't. But it wouldn't stop them doing their level best.

Her attention was caught by motion at the top of the church. Katie saw it at the same time as she grabbed her arm.

"Ellen, did you see that?"

"What?"

Katie pointed over at Alicia. The girl, wearing a thunderous expression, was marching toward Charlie Staunton. Katie gave Danny to Ellen and moved as quickly as her skirts allowed. She didn't manage to reach Alicia in time.

"How dare you? Take your hands off him." Alicia pulled the child closer to her away from Charlie's reach. "What were you looking in his mouth for? He is not an animal but a child."

"Miss, do yourself a favor and leave me to choose a boy. I aim to get me a healthy boy who can work on my farm. I ain't providing food and board for someone who can't work."

"The idea is to provide a home." Alicia's cultured accent seemed to have some effect on Staunton. He wasn't shouting back at her, something he wouldn't fail to do if it were Ellen or Katie taking him to task.

"William is a healthy strong individual. He is also a child of nine. He deserves a home with a mother and father. A chance of a decent future. Not to be worked to death by some jumped up overseer."

Charlie Staunton turned purple at the insult but before he could respond, Mrs. Grey swooped in.

"Alicia, darling, have you met my friend Mrs. Shaw? This is the delightful young lady I spoke to you about. Her mama was a real beauty back in the day. Grew up on the Summerfield Planation."

Ellen chuckled as she came to stand behind Katie. "I could almost feel sorry for Mrs. Shaw. Mrs. Grey has her mesmerized. Charlie Staunton has been put in his place too. I am enjoying today."

"We aren't here to enjoy ourselves, Ellen. What are we going to do with all these children? Aaron was right, some people just want cheap labor."

"Don't you go believing the decent folk of Clover Springs will behave like Staunton. That man is a creep." Ellen gave Katie's arm a squeeze. "Don't forget the weather isn't helping. There may be some people on the outlying ranches who would love to help. But they can't get into town. Little Beaver says some of the snow drifts are very deep so people are likely to remain at home."

"But I promised all the children would have a home by Christmas. How am I going to keep that promise?" Katie said, her voice muffled by the tears she was struggling to hold back.

"You promised them a home not parents. So, the children who don't get adopted will live at Hope House for the time being at least. We can provide them with love and a good safe Christmas. In the new year, when spring breaks, more families might come forward. Or Father Molloy may be able to find suitable families back in Boston."

"Will we have enough funds to last till spring?"

"We will, have some faith. Remember Mam always told us to count our blessings."

"Speaking of Mam, I wonder if Liam will come to visit us. Daddy hinted he would in his last letter. I still can't believe he is home safe in Galway. I wonder if he has found Siobhan yet? Maybe she is already married."

"Katie, would you stop worrying. We have enough to deal with without bringing more trouble to our door."

"Since when have you become so grown up?" Katie said, poking Ellen in the ribs. "It used to be me reassuring you."

"After all we have been through in the last few years, sister dear, I believe we can face anything so long as we are together. Now why don't we go rescue Alicia from Mrs. Shaw."

"Do we have to? You know how much I despise that woman."

"You and me both but poor Alicia doesn't deserve to be left at her mercy. I wonder why Mrs. Grey insisted on introducing them. Next thing you know she will be inviting them over for tea."

Ellen nearly choked on her own words as they heard Mrs. Grey issue precisely that invitation. Ellen couldn't look at Katie for fear she would laugh. Alicia looked as if she wished she could be anywhere else but it was the glow of mischief in Mrs. Grey's eyes Ellen found particularly interesting. The older woman was up to something.

* * *

Aaron walked Ellen back to the orphanage. Or at least that is what he pretended he was doing. He wanted to see Alicia. He had been tempted to step in when she had taken Charlie Staunton to task, but instead he had watched in admiration as she put the horrible man in his place. He was about to congratulate her when Mrs. Grey had moved to speak to Alicia, almost dragging Mrs. Shaw behind her. He listened as she extended an invitation to tea. *Say no, Alicia, please.* But his unspoken plea went unanswered as Alicia nodded her head in acceptance. How could she want to be in the same room as Mrs. Shaw and her equally horrid friend Ida Hawthorn? She doesn't know them. But Mrs. Grey does. Aaron caught Ellen's speculative glance at her friend. Maybe Ellen suspected the old lady was up to something too. Whatever it was, Aaron wasn't positive Alicia wouldn't end up getting hurt. His urge to protect her came back in full force once more. He barely knew the girl yet he spent more time caring about how she was getting on than he did thinking about his new mail order bride and the homestead he should be preparing for her.

CHAPTER 22

"Miss Carstairs, how delighted I am to make your acquaintance. Mrs. Grey, thank you for inviting us to tea." Ida Hawthorn took a dainty sip of tea. "We rarely have such illustrious company in Clover Springs. You must think us terribly backward."

"Not at all. I like your town. It's..."

"Quaint," Ida tittered, her laugh grating on Alicia's nerves. "So tell me, Miss Carstairs, is it true your mother was presented to Queen Victoria?"

"My grandmother," Alicia corrected softly.

"Oh I see. She must be a "Lady" then? Perhaps she would know members of my own family. They too have been presented at Court."

"My grandmother died when my mother was a young girl. I never met her."

"Oh."

The disappointment on the other woman's face amused Alicia but she was aware of Mrs. Grey watching her closely.

"Did your mother grow up in England? I would love to live there. So civilized don't you think?"

"I wouldn't know. I have never been. My mother grew up just outside Atlanta. Her father owned a plantation and she lived there until just before the war. She met my father, married and moved to Boston."

"How awful it must be to watch your whole life disintegrate. I always thought it would be fun to live on a plantation. Having servants to cater to your every whim."

"Really, I should think I would get bored very quickly." Alicia almost bit her tongue. She shouldn't have spoken so tartly.

Ida Hawthorn's eyes bulged. Alicia could feel her mother's disapproval at her honesty. But Mama wasn't here anymore and she was done pretending. There was nothing she hated more than being dressed up and having to behave like a china doll. If she'd been born a man, she could have become a lawyer, maybe even saved her father's practice. She certainly wouldn't be sitting here drinking tea with this awful woman. She hadn't enjoyed these types of social occasions in Boston but at least there the attention had been focused on her pretty mother. Here she had nobody to hide behind.

She wished she was out riding with Little Beaver and the children. She was helping teach the younger ones to ride and they loved it. This afternoon was perfect for being outdoors, although a little cold, the sky was clear. Reluctantly, she dragged her attention back to Mrs. Grey's sitting room. She smoothed down her skirt yet again wondering what she should talk about.

"When will you be returning to Boston, Miss Carstairs?" Mrs. Shaw asked, her beady eyes looking at Alicia as if knowing she was a fraud.

"Well, I'm not sure. I promised to stay with the children for a while. I guess I will leave sometime in the spring. Father Molloy said the weather is likely to make travel difficult for some time."

"How can you live in that orphanage? A lady with your class and breeding being surrounded by all those children. Who knows what backgrounds they come from." Ida Hawthorn barely took a breath before continuing. "I was against the orphanage from the start. Clover Springs used to be a respectable place until that priest arrived with his ideas."

"It wasn't just the priest, dear," Mrs. Shaw murmured.

"No he had support from those awful mail order

brides. We haven't had anything other than problems since they arrived. Katie Sullivan, she may think highly of herself but she was engaged to another man when she met Daniel Sullivan."

"Disgraceful it was. He was a train robber, and nearly killed the whole town."

"Now ladies stop exaggerating. Katie Sullivan wasn't to know and she was helpful in catching the group," Mrs. Grey said.

"Only when they threatened our town," Mrs. Shaw muttered.

"Katie Sullivan and her friends have stolen all the single men in the town. We didn't need them to come here."

"Now, Ida, what have I told you before? You will find someone special." Mrs. Shaw flustered.

"I find the ladies in Clover Springs charming. They have been very pleasant to me," Alicia said, ignoring the urge to itch the back of her neck. How much longer would she have to stay before it would be polite to leave?

"Have you met Emer Shipley? She grew up with a bunch of outlaws for goodness sake and now she is married to the richest man in Clover Springs. I feel sorry for poor Mrs. Shipley."

"Why? Is he ugly? Is she unhappy in her marriage?" Alicia chose to deliberately misunderstand the woman's remark. She spotted an approving look from Mrs. Grey before it was quickly masked. She allowed herself a small smile but couldn't let it widen at the look on Miss Hawthorn's face. She was almost purple.

"I meant Mrs. Shipley, Lawrence's mother. You must have met her in Boston. She is a queen of society."

"Yes, we have met."

"Then you can guess what it meant to have her son lower himself to marry someone so, so…"

"Unsuitable." Mrs. Shaw finished Miss Hawthorn's comment as the younger woman seemed to be incapable.

Alicia's nails dug into the palm of her hands. She knew Lawrence's mother, Mrs. Shipley. She had been a regular visitor at her mother's tea parties. The same woman had cut her dead once word broke about her father. She could still feel the shame of holding her hand out in greeting to the old witch who had walked on by. As if they never met.

"Frankly, I think I feel sorry for Emer marrying into that family. She must be brave or else she loves her husband very much." Alicia ignored Mrs. Shaw's and Miss Hawthorn's reaction. She wasn't in Boston anymore so why pretend she was. From now on, she was going to be the person she wanted to be.

"I am happy to say it's both. Emer Shipley is our

town nurse and has already been credited with saving at least one person's life. She and Lawrence and their twins are as happy as any family could be."

Thrilled with Mrs. Grey's support, Alicia added. "I have only met her briefly but she seemed like a charming girl," Alicia said, not looking at either Mrs. Shaw or Miss Hawthorn.

An awkward silence ensued. The clock pendulum swung back and forth as Alicia tried to think of a reason to leave. She didn't want to offend Mrs. Grey but at the same time she's had enough of the other two ladies.

"Perhaps it was time I was going. There is a lot to do at the orphanage," Alicia said, setting her tea cup on the tray in front of her. Mrs. Shaw seemed reluctant to see her go.

"Ida, did you hear Father Molloy is expecting all the townsfolk to adopt his orphans. The audacity of the man. How dare he expect us to offer shelter to a stranger?"

"We knew this was coming. Ever since the first mention of an orphanage in Clover Springs. They are ruining the reputation of this whole town."

Alicia's patience was spent. "I would have thought it was your Christian duty to look after children especially those as nice as the ones at Clover Springs. They can't help not having parents."

"We don't know their backgrounds." Ida sniffed dabbing her mouth with her hanky.

"They are children not thoroughbred horses. Who cares what their backgrounds are?" Alicia burst out passionately. "They are innocents and deserve, at the very least, a chance to make a good life."

"Well said, Alicia." Mrs. Grey's approving look made Alicia sit straighter. "Ida Hawthorn, you should be ashamed of yourself. It's almost Christmas, the season of goodwill to mankind. Jesus himself asked people to be nice to children."

"Yes, well... I can't be expected to provide a home for a child. Not when I am not married." Miss Hawthorn sniffed.

"No, I can see your difficulty, Miss Hawthorn, but perhaps you would consider it Mrs. Shaw. You have a fine house and the financial ability to provide a good home. Wouldn't your son like a sister or brother?" Alicia had to cover her laugh with a cough at the look on Mrs. Shaw's face.

"Ida, is that the time? Goodness me, I promised Mr. Shaw I would make his favorite pie. Please excuse us, Mrs. Grey. Miss Carstairs." Mrs. Shaw couldn't get out of the house quickly enough.

CHAPTER 23

As the door closed, Alicia exchanged a look with Mrs. Grey before they both burst out laughing.

"You are a wicked girl, Alicia. I knew your family. I too grew up in the South. I remember going to Summerfield dances. Your father was a wonderful horseman, he competed in every race. Your grandfather held a tournament every summer. The winner could choose a lady as the queen of the ball."

Alicia leaned in eagerly. Her parents had spoken of how they met but it was different hearing it from another person who had been present.

"That's how my father met my mother. Did you know her?" she asked.

"Only to exchange pleasantries. I have to admit we didn't see eye to eye on many subjects." Mrs. Grey didn't quite meet Alicia's eyes but she sensed it wasn't from shame. *She doesn't want to embarrass me.*

"Oh. I wasn't aware my mother held strong views about anything other than looking beautiful and behaving like a lady." Alicia bit her tongue. She couldn't believe she had just criticized her dead mother to a stranger. "I apologize. I shouldn't have spoken out of turn."

"Your mother was typical of her class. *My* class. We were reared to consider beauty as a prized possession. It was to be our main goal. That and marrying well."

"I take it, from what you have said, you rebelled against that notion."

"Well, I was never what you would consider an easy child. My mother would have preferred a daughter like your mother. She was the perfect child before turning into a real Southern belle. My mother was obsessed with your mother's family. Summerfield Plantation was one of the biggest in the country. At one point, your family owned about 300 slaves."

"What about you, Mrs. Grey. You said you weren't the model daughter. You didn't go off fighting in the war?"

Mrs. Grey laughed. "No, I was never the model daughter. My family owned slaves too. Plantations as big as ours couldn't survive without them. My father was considered a fair master. He didn't mistreat his people, well apart from holding them in bondage. But from a Southern perspective they were well treated. I spent a lot of time down in the slave quarters. I taught anyone who wanted to learn how to read and write. I figured they would need those skills if they ever did get their freedom."

"Was your father annoyed with you?"

"I didn't tell him. I knew he wouldn't approve. But it was worth it. I met David because of my work with the slaves. He was one of those brave men and women who helped the slaves to escape."

"You helped your father's slaves to run away?"

Mrs. Grey looked down at her hands. "I couldn't bear not to. I can still remember the cries as families were torn apart."

"You said your father treated them well."

"He did by the standards of his day but he still separated families. He would sell the female children as he wanted more men in the fields. I had to help keep some of those families together."

"So did you run away with David?" Alicia leaned forward in her chair finding the story fascinating.

"No, and that is something I regret to this day. Never let anyone or anything stand in the way of your happiness, Alicia. You never know what tomorrow brings."

Stunned by the sadness on the older woman's face,

Alicia surprised both of them by moving closer and taking her hand. "Was David caught trying to help slaves run away?"

Mrs. Grey took a few minutes to answer.

"No, he wasn't and he didn't lose one single person. They all made it to Canada to freedom. Thanks, in part, to David and the other wonderful people on the underground railway." Mrs. Grey had a faraway look in her eyes. She was lost in her memories. Alicia was content to sit patiently in silence. She was surprised by how much she enjoyed Mrs. Grey's company. It was so unusual to find anyone approving of her and not correcting her for being too manly in her outlook or not sitting straight enough or whatever fault her mother's society friends could find.

"Did your father find out about the part you played in the escapes?"

"No, never. War broke out and he was too busy with that to notice anything about his daughter. Well, at least until I insisted on leaving the plantation and moving to Richmond. I became a nurse. Not a real one of course, I mean I didn't have any proper training, although we learnt very quickly." Mrs. Grey's eyes were shadowed with pain.

"Was it as bad as they say?" Alicia whispered.

"It was worse. There are no words to describe the conditions we worked in. Many of those mutilated young men had been left for hours after being injured. They were in a dreadful state by the time they got to us. We didn't have sufficient medicines or knowledge. There were many so-called surgeons, many of them Irish, who should never have been allowed near a human being. It was horrible."

"I'm sorry, I shouldn't have asked."

"You are right to be curious."

"Did your parents finally accept what you did?"

"No, they didn't. The last conversation I had with my father was when he gave me an ultimatum. I could choose working in the hospital or coming home. I chose the hospital. He went home."

"Did you ever reconcile?"

Mrs. Grey shook her head. Alicia sensed she needed a few minutes to deal with her memories. She stared into the fire allowing Mrs. Grey to regain her composure.

"My being arrested as a spy ended whatever chance we had of reconciliation."

"You were a spy?" Alicia didn't hide her shock.

"I didn't consider myself a spy then and I certainly don't now but I can see where others got their opinion. There was a prison holding prisoners of war, Yankee soldiers near the hospital where I worked. One of the doctors was given permission to visit the prison to provide medical aid to the Yankee officers. I went with him. The conditions those men lived in were horrific. I was appalled and became convinced I had a duty to help them in any way possible. I believe God led me to that prison. David was there."

"The man who had helped the slaves?"

Mrs. Grey nodded, taking a deep breath before she continued with her story. "David was a doctor. He stayed behind with some wounded men and ended up being captured. I couldn't lose him again. I begged the doctor from our hospital to take me with him on every visit. I brought extra clothes and food, both to bribe the guards and to give to David. I smuggled in whatever medicine I could buy."

"Did he survive the war?" Alicia whispered, sensing Mrs. Grey didn't often talk about this period of her life.

"No. Although maybe he could have," Mrs. Grey whispered, a tear escaping from her eye.

CHAPTER 24

Alicia wanted to hug Mrs. Grey but resisted the urge. Instead, she kept rubbing her hand. "Please don't tell me anymore. I hate seeing you so upset."

"No, it's important I tell you. I don't want anyone else to live a lifetime of regret for not taking a chance on someone they love. I should have gone with David that last time he came to help some more of the slaves escape. If I had been braver, I would have had some time with the man I loved. Maybe I could have stopped him going to war."

"From what you said, I doubt it. It sounds like David was driven by a need to help humanity. I don't think a person like that would have been content to sit on the sidelines."

"Perhaps you are right. We will never know."

"So he died in the prison."

Mrs. Grey nodded, as she pressed a hanky to her eyes.

"The prisoners had planned an escape. Conditions were deteriorating. It wasn't just those who were locked up who were suffering. The people of Richmond suffered badly from the blockade. Southern families were starving so there wasn't much food or sympathy for Yankee prisoners. David and a couple of the other officers decided they had to make a break for freedom."

Alicia sat listening in horrified fascination. She couldn't imagine what those poor men had endured.

"David was supposed to be in the first group of prisoners to escape but at the last minute, he let another man go in his place. This man, by all accounts, had been suicidal and David must have felt he wouldn't survive the prison life for much longer. The escape was a success. Close to twenty of David's friends made it back to the North."

"And David?"

"He was shot while attempting to escape." Mrs. Grey's eyes filled with tears. "I was allowed to see him but there was nothing we could do. The doctor married us. David survived long enough to say I do."

"Oh, Mrs. Grey I am so sorry. I don't know what to say to you."

"It was an Irishman who shot him. He laughed in my face as he related the details of the escape attempt. He came into the cell where David was one of the few remaining men and shot them all. He didn't bother to hide it. I hated him and all Irish people for a long time after that."

Silence lingered. Alicia couldn't think of something to say to make Mrs. Grey feel better. She wanted to cry for David and their lost love, but that wouldn't help the older woman. She waited for Mrs. Grey to recover her composure.

"Alicia, don't make the same mistake I made. When the Irish girls came here first, I hated them. I was horrible to Katie and young Ellen. She was only twelve, a child, yet I treated her as less than a human being. All because of that Irish Captain who murdered David. Ellen has a way of working herself into your heart. She is a very special person. Her sister Katie is another wonderful lady. Give them a chance. Get to know them as people first before you judge them for being Irish."

Alicia looked away. She didn't know what to say. "Papa always said the Irish were a nation of drunken fighters."

"It's not important what your father believed. It is what you believe that matters. Has Ellen or any of the others ever given you reason to believe what your father told you?"

Alicia shook her head. "I think my parents were wrong about a lot of things." She bit her lip wondering if she should continue. Mrs. Grey didn't say anything. She seemed to be waiting for an explanation.

"I can't help feeling if my parents hadn't been so insistent on my being a lady, I would be better able to take care of myself now." Alicia sniffed. "I sound very sorry for myself. Please excuse me."

"You sound like someone who has found herself doubting the way she was brought up. What happened to your father?"

Alicia wasn't sure what made her tell the truth. "He killed himself after it was alleged he had stolen money from his clients. He wasn't prepared to face the scandal."

"Oh, you poor girl. You were left to deal with that."

"I wasn't sure what was going on at first as nobody would tell me. They kept dismissing me because I am a girl. My fiancé, I should say ex-fiancé decided I should leave Boston. He said it was best for all concerned. He dealt with the financial arrangements." She wasn't about to admit to Robert's role in securing her governess position with Mr. Oaks.

"Were you allowed to keep anything?"

"A few weeks before he died, my father gave me the

family bible. He was acting very strangely, kept telling me not to show it to anyone. He said I should leave Boston and go to stay with Mother's family. But I didn't know them so I wouldn't go. He got quite angry but eventually he saw I wasn't going to leave him. So I have that and my personal belongings which amounted to a few dresses and some trinkets. I was told the sale of the house, the horses and everything else wouldn't be enough to pay off all Papa's debts. I didn't want anything anyway. Father stole from everyone even those who couldn't afford it. If it had just been his rich clients, I may have understood. He stole from people who couldn't pay their own bills." Alicia wiped away a tear. "Why would you steal from the poor? Some of those people didn't have enough money to pay for food or medical attention. I can't blame them for being angry."

"Yes they are right to be angry but you are not the correct target of that anger. You were an innocent victim too."

"I was advised to leave Boston. I found a job but I think you know about that."

Mrs. Grey patted her hand. "Thank goodness Father Molloy was on that train."

Alicia didn't say anything. She couldn't bear to think of what could have happened if she had traveled on to Leadville.

"Although from what I have heard, it was an act of charity that brought you to the attention of Father Molloy."

"It was nothing. I couldn't let that woman mistreat Harry."

"It takes courage to stand up for your convictions, particularly when in a vulnerable situation. You are not responsible for your parents' actions or opinions only your own."

"I would like to find a way to pay back the people Papa stole from. But I am not sure how." Alicia shook. "I don't have anything of value."

"You may never have sufficient cash to repay his debts but you can make amends in other ways. You can choose to live a different life to that of your parents. There are many people who could benefit from knowing you, Alicia. Those children at the orphanage for example."

"I don't know what I can do for them." Alicia whispered.

"Be their friend. Never underestimate the value of friendship, particularly to those who have never known it. Those children need someone strong and compassionate to help them adjust to their new life. You are just that person, Alicia, if you want to be. You have already begun to let go of your parents' prejudices. Develop a belief system of your own." Mrs. Grey smiled. "If I can at my age, anyone can."

Alicia couldn't speak. Mrs. Grey hugged her before pushing her blonde hair back from her face.

"Alicia, don't let other people dictate what type of life you lead. Listen to your heart. Trust your instinct. Above all, remember you have friends now who will stick by you no matter what. Your family may have let you down, but your friends here in Clover Springs won't. I promise you that. The town is a real community now. The people here look after each other. The girls are the reason for that. Katie, Ellen and all their friends."

Alicia stayed silent. She was too choked up to speak.

"I guess I can talk all day about how wonderful Clover Springs and its inhabitants are. Well, most of them. Thankfully they are not all like our tea companions."

"Why did you invite them?" Alicia asked tentatively hoping she wouldn't upset Mrs. Grey.

"I wanted you to hear them saying things you had said." Mrs. Grey looked at her before continuing. "I suspected you had never really thought about the attitudes you hold. I suppose I hoped, if you heard them being petty, small minded and mean you may..."

"See just how horrible a person I am?" Alicia didn't quite manage to hide her anger.

"No dear. I don't believe you to be a horrible person. If I did, I would never have invited you. I believe you have yet to develop your own view of the world. I happen to believe it is impossible for someone with such a kind heart to be so cruel."

CHAPTER 25

"Aaron, a letter came for you today. It's from Boston. Thought you might want it in a hurry." Katie's eyes twinkled with curiosity. She was dying to know what was in the letter. He almost gave it to her to read.

Opening it, he read it slowly.

"Says Mrs. Gantley has found me a match."

"Oh that's wonderful. Your ma will be so pleased. What's her name?"

Aaron had to look at the letter again, the name hadn't registered. *What is wrong with you? You wanted a mail order bride. Now you got one.*

I want Alicia.

"What's wrong? Aaron?" Katie's puzzled tone intruded on his thoughts.

"Here, you read it. I got to get over to see Samuel."

Aaron knew Katie thought he had lost his head but he had to speak to his brother. What was he going to do? He couldn't bring a girl halfway across the country when his heart belonged elsewhere. That wouldn't be fair. To either of them.

* * *

ALICIA WALKED out the door of the orphanage stopping when she heard Aaron's voice. Her heart beat faster. He was here again. Was it to see her? Could she take Mrs. Grey's advice? She couldn't tell him how she felt but there were ways of letting a man know you were interested. How she wished she had paid more attention to her mother now. Her mother would have known how to conquer Aaron's heart.

"Mrs. Gantley wrote back. She's found me a bride."

Alicia stood still, her heart beating so fast and loud she was sure they would hear her. But they continued walking toward the barn. She waited until they had gone inside before making her way quickly to the gate. Closing it behind her, she walked slowly to the school.

Aaron was going to marry a mail order bride. Someone he had never met. He obviously didn't like her. She must have misread the signs.

With downcast eyes, she barely acknowledged the people she met on the boardwalk. She spotted Ida

Hawthorn walking on the other side of the street. She hoped the woman would continue walking. Her day was bad enough already.

She couldn't believe the young woman shared the views she held when she first came here. How could someone who spent time around wonderful people like Wilma and Little Beaver be so narrow minded. It was different for her; she hadn't known real Indians. Only read about them in the paper. That's just an excuse. You wouldn't judge a white stranger badly. How shallow she'd been. Somewhere along the way, she had turned into a replica of her mother. Only without the fancy clothes, the nice house and the money. Not to mention the adoring husband. Papa had loved her mother so much. What would it be like if Aaron would look at her like Papa had looked at Mama? That was never going to happen.

CHAPTER 26

As Alicia neared the school, she saw a crowd gathered outside. She pushed back the bad feeling she had, trying to breathe deeply and stay calm.

She spotted Bertram Shaw standing alone.

"What's going on?"

"Some of the children are gone."

"Gone where?"

Bertram wouldn't look at her making her more nervous. "Where are Steven and Harry?"

Bertram looked everywhere but at her face. "I asked you a question."

"They ran off; Rosa went with them. They will be back; they are just looking for attention."

She spotted Ellen speaking to the sheriff. She walked quickly, but carefully, not wanting to slip on the icy surface. "Bertram told me Steven and Harry ran off."

Tears ran down Ellen's face. "Yes they did and Rosa went with them. I didn't know anything had happened at recess. I sent John back to Wilma with a message and he only discovered his sister missing when he came back. I thought she had gone with him."

"Don't cry Ellen, you can't keep an eye on all the children. There are simply too many of them. What can I do?"

"Find Little Beaver. He'll be at Hope House with the horses. He is the best chance. He can track anything."

Heart racing, Alicia went to find Little Beaver. Instead she found Aaron.

"Where's Little Beaver?"

"He's gone home to Asha. Nandita sent word their baby will make an arrival very soon." Aaron smiled but his smile faded at the look in her eyes. "What's wrong?"

"Some of the children ran away from school. Ellen thought Little Beaver could find them. They've been gone a while."

Aaron turned in the direction of the stables.

Wringing her hands, she moved to follow him but he stopped her.

"Where are you going? You can't go for a ride. Not

today. Look at that sky. There is going to be more snow."

"Steven, Harry and Rosa ran away from the school. I must help find them. Steven can't talk. They must be very scared by now," Alicia protested but it was no use. "I ride as well as you do." *If not better.*

"Miss Carstairs, please leave this to the men."

Alicia almost stamped her feet in frustration. Why did the fact she was female always cause problems? She didn't attempt to follow him but went into the orphanage and changed into her riding skirt. Maybe he would change his mind when he saw she was determined to help. She couldn't sit here doing nothing.

* * *

When she arrived back at the school a small crowd of adults had gathered. They were discussing what to do in Little Beaver's absence.

"We can't afford to wait for more help. That sky is full of snow. We need to get the kids back before dark," Lawrence Shipley stated. The sheriff agreed.

"We need to split up. Aaron, you head out toward your homestead, Shipley you go east. I will stay center. Take a couple of men with you. Don't split up. I don't want to have to send out another search party for any stragglers."

"Best take some hot coffee and spare blankets with you. Those children aren't dressed for a hike in the snow," Ellen said, distress making her voice tremble.

Alicia inched closer to Aaron hoping he'd changed his mind.

"Miss Carstairs, you stay home with the other women. I don't have time to babysit you today."

Tears pricked her eyes at his curt tone.

"Come on, Alicia, you can help us with the other children. The men will be back before you know it."

Reluctantly, Alicia walked her horse back to the orphanage. On entering the stable, she heard someone crying. Moving quietly, she discovered John face down in the straw.

"John, sweetheart, it will be alright. The men will find them."

"No they won't. Rosa's my little sister. I should have been there to protect her. I'm going to lose her too. "

"No you are not. Stop thinking like that. They will find her, I promise."

But the boy was too heartbroken to listen to her. She clenched and unclenched her hands. Surely she was better out there searching for the children than staying here waiting for news.

"John, I am going to try to find them. Do you have any idea where Rosa might go?"

"One of the kids said Bertram was really nasty to her. She may have gone to her secret place."

Alicia's hopes rose. "Where is that, John?"

"I don't know. She said it was too secret to share. But it is probably near the river. Rosa likes to listen to the sound the water makes. Says it reminds her a little of the sea. Daddy used to take us for walks down the beach when we were little. I don't think Rosa remembers really as she was just a baby."

Alicia knew where the river was. Little Beaver had pointed it out to Alicia on her rides. She was sure it wouldn't take long to find the children. Soon they would be back in Clover Springs.

You shouldn't go alone. I must. The men have already left and I can't ask Ellen to come with me. She shouldn't be riding in her condition.

Giving John a quick hug, she led the horse back out of the stables and away from the orphanage. When she was far enough away, she mounted and headed out in the direction of the river. If she took the trail Little Beaver had shown her, she may catch up with Aaron. The river was quite near his homestead. She may even reach the river before him.

CHAPTER 27

Alicia kept riding and calling the children by name but there was no sign of them. She started praying, hoping that one of the other adults had found them. Just as she was about to turn back toward the town, she saw something up ahead. She urged the horse into a canter.

Harry was screaming Steven's name by the side of the river. She tried to see what he was looking at but couldn't. Heart beating, she jumped off the horse remembering to tie it to the tree in case it ran off. She moved quickly to the river's edge. Rosa was the furthest out, lying on top of some ice, clinging to a branch of a tree. Alarmed, Alicia noticed the big crack in the ice right behind the child. Steven was sitting closer to the bank but given the stricken look on his face, Alicia guessed he was frozen with terror. Harry put his foot on the ice but Alicia grabbed him back.

"Let me go. He's my brother." Harry struggled kicking out with both feet. She held him tighter.

"You will only make the ice crack more. You could cause both to fall into the water. They won't last long, it's too cold." The stubborn expression on his face didn't bode well. "Harry, I can't worry about you as well. Aaron should be along any minute. Why don't you go see if you can see him?" The boy hesitated, looking between his brother and the trail behind them. "Go on. We need Aaron's help."

Muttering what sounded like an oath, Harry walked toward the trail. Alicia looked back at the children. Biting her lip, she knew she had to act quickly but if she ventured on to the ice, it would likely crack.

"Children listen to me. You both need to move slowly toward me. Steven, you first."

Steven shook his head.

"He won't move, Miss Alicia. I think he is afraid to leave me alone."

"I will help you in a minute, Rosa, but first we need Steven to get off the ice. It won't carry the weight of both of you. Do you understand me, Steven? If you don't come back to me, Rosa will fall into the cold water."

Alicia didn't like scaring the child but it was the

only hope of reaching him. "Lie flat down and inch your way toward me. I will grab you and pull you free."

Alicia lay down on the bank, with most of her weight on the ground, she reached both hands over the ice. Her intention being to grab Steven as soon as he came close enough and pull him to safety. It took a few seconds but Steven eventually did as instructed. Her heart was in her mouth as the child moved slowly toward her. Finally, he was close enough to her hands for her to grab him and pull him closer. She tore off her coat and wrapped it around the shivering child.

"Wait up there near the horse."

The boy looked from her face to where Rosa clung to the branch.

"Go, Steven. I will help Rosa better if I know you are safe."

Steven walked toward the horse. Alicia scanned her surroundings. How was she going to rescue Rosa? It started to snow again, falling quickly.

"Rosa, I need you to lie flat out on the snow like Steven did. It will distribute your weight. Can you do that?"

"I don't think so, Miss Alicia." Rosa's voice quivered. "I don't want to let the branch go."

"Sweetheart, I am going to try to come nearer to you." The ice nearest the bank looked thicker than out where Rosa was. She hoped she was right. She couldn't swim, not that she fancied her chances of moving in such cold water. But she couldn't not help the child either.

She braced herself as she moved slowly onto the ice. She did just as she had instructed Steven to do and crawled along the surface. As she got nearer to Rosa, they heard an ominous crack. Rosa screamed as the ice around her started to break up.

"Rosa, look at me, don't look at the ice." Alicia commanded. She thought she heard someone shouting at her from the bank of the river but she didn't want to take her eyes off Rosa.

"Rosa, you have to let the branch go now and come closer to me."

"I can't." Rosa started crying. "I'm scared."

"I know you are but you have to trust me. Let the branch go and lie down on the ice just like Steven did. He got back to the bank and you will too. Please."

Alicia inched closer but hearing some noises she guessed she better not move any closer. "Rosa, you need to be a big girl and do this for me. John is so upset you went away. We need to get back home to him, okay?"

Rosa nodded, her hand moving slowly off the branch.

"That's it. Move very slowly and don't look behind you."

Alicia stretched her hands as much as she could. She was within a fingertip's distance of Rosa. "Almost have you, can you move a little closer to me. Put your hand out to reach mine."

The ice boomed beneath them. "Don't worry Rosa the ice will make noises. It doesn't mean it's not safe." Alicia hoped her words proved true. She waited until Rosa was a little closer and then pulled the girl towards her. She was so busy concentrating on Rosa she didn't realize anyone was behind her until they grabbed her ankles.

"Hold onto Rosa and I will pull you both out."

Relief surged through her body as Aaron's strong hands encircled her ankles. She held tight to Rosa as both moved back across the ice to the bank. Soon their ordeal was over. She was hugging Rosa, and Aaron had his arms around both of them. Harry held Steven beside them.

"You are freezing. We need to get out of this snowstorm. My homestead is closest."

Alicia didn't argue. She didn't have the energy. Anyway, Aaron knew the area better than she did. Now that both children were safe, her limbs were shaking and wouldn't stop. She tried without success to mount her horse. Her wet clothes hindered her efforts.

Aaron helped her to mount, his strong arms encircling her waist. He then picked Rosa up and put her in front of Alicia. The girl cuddled close.

"I will carry both boys with me. Harry is old enough to hang onto my back. Steven will travel in the front. It isn't far. Stay near as I don't want to lose you."

Alicia nodded, not capable of speaking. She couldn't remember ever being so cold. She closed her eyes briefly before forcing them open. Falling asleep wasn't an option.

CHAPTER 28

Aaron was right, it didn't take long to get to his homestead, although it felt like hours. He put both horses in the barn. "I will come out and look after them in a few minutes. I need to get a fire going to warm you up. I don't want the children getting a chill."

Alicia knew she should be more helpful but her limbs were so heavy, it took all her energy to follow him into the house, half pulling, half dragging Rosa with her.

Aaron worked quickly and soon had a small fire going in the hearth. He rummaged through some drawers on the other side of the room and took out some dry clothes. "They won't fit but you best get out of those wet clothes. All of you."

His eyes met Alicia's as heat flooded through her. She couldn't wear a shirt or whatever it was that lay on the bed. It wasn't decent.

"It might not be decent," he said surprising her by reading her thoughts so accurately. "But would you prefer to be decent or dead?"

Alicia knew he was right. Aaron picked the smallest sizes for Steven and Rosa but the garments were still way too big on them. Alicia helped by folding back the sleeves. There was nothing they could do about the length.

"I am going out to check the horses. Boys turn your back and allow Miss Alicia to get dressed. The water should be boiled by the time I get back."

He indicated the pot he had set on the fire. "The stove hasn't come yet so we must manage."

"We won't be here that long."

"Don't be too sure of that, Miss Alicia. This snowstorm could last a day or a week."

Alicia knew she had gone pale as the blood flooded to her toes. She couldn't stay here for a week. The townspeople would be worried. John would think the worst about Rosa. She had to get back to town.

"Change first before you make any decisions, please." Aaron smiled at her. She colored again realizing he seemed to be able to read her exact thoughts. *Not all of them I hope.*

* * *

THE CHILDREN GIGGLED when she changed into a pair of Aaron's britches and a cotton shirt. Both were way too big for her, so she had to fold up the sleeves and the pants. She needed some string to secure them on the waist but she didn't see any lying around. She didn't feel comfortable enough to go looking through Aaron's things.

She told the children to get into the bed. They needed to get warm and the fire was taking too long.

Aaron returned and heated up some of the coffee Ellen had given him. There was no milk but the warm liquid was just what she needed. She added some cold water to the drink before giving it to the children. "It will help you warm up from the inside."

"Don't know why adults drink coffee. It's disgusting," Rosa complained.

"I know, darling, but it will help keep you well. I don't want you getting sick."

"Thank you, Miss Alicia, for coming onto the ice to get me. I think you are very brave."

"She's something alright but I am not sure brave covers it," Aaron snarled.

"I couldn't stand there and do nothing," She protested but went quiet at the glare he sent her.

"We will talk about that later. I need to go find us

something to eat. I didn't come prepared for a camp out."

Alicia moved to the window. Looking out she could see it was still snowing but it didn't look as heavy as before.

"Could we not try to make it back to town? It would be best for everyone," she asked but sensed the answer would be no.

"No. It's too dangerous. You and the children have suffered enough today. We don't know how long it will keep snowing. It could turn into a blizzard. We are best waiting here."

"But if it does become a blizzard, you will be in danger too?"

"I know my way around this area. I won't go far. A hot meal will make us all feel better." His voice sounded confident but she saw the concern in his eyes. She guessed he was trying not to alarm the children.

"Be careful. Please," she said softly. If he heard her, he gave no sign as he closed the door behind him blocking out the snow storm. Shivering she sat closer to the fire. The children had fallen asleep, worn out by their experiences she guessed. She longed for a hot bath and warm bed. The fire wasn't giving out enough heat for her cold bones.

Time passed slowly. She added wood to the fire

before looking for something to eat. Given the weather, Aaron might not find any food. She found some canned items. Peaches and some other fruits. The children would be delighted.

CHAPTER 29

Rosa whimpered in her sleep prompting Alicia to check on them. Relieved they weren't running a fever, Alicia wrapped the blankets around the three sleeping children. Staring at their innocent faces, she wondered what the next few years would hold for them. Who would adopt Harry and Steven? Would they keep the brothers together? Seeing Harry holding Steven's hand while asleep made her eyes water. Separating those children would be cruel but judging from the comments Father Molloy and the others had made, it often happened. Siblings were separated and some never met up again. She couldn't let that happen.

What can you do to stop it? They aren't going to let a single woman adopt one child never mind two. But they would if I was married.

* * *

Time passed very slowly. She huddled closer to the small fire in the hearth trying to ignore the occasional animal sounds coming from outside. Where was Aaron? She prayed he would find some food but more importantly he would come back safe. Thinking she heard something she moved to the window but the heavy snowfall blocked her view.

Sometime later the children woke up. Harry moved toward the window. “Looks like Mr. Higgins was right. The snow is coming down very heavily now. Where is he?”

“He went to get some food. He will be back soon,” Alicia answered.

“Miss Carstairs, do you think we will be home for Christmas?”

"I certainly hope so Rosa, we have a few days to go yet." Alicia wasn’t at all sure if they would ever see Clover Springs again. Aaron had been gone a long time. What if he got lost? Or was injured? Or dead?

"Father Christmas won’t know where we are. Wilma said he would leave us presents if we were good. I've tried to be very good this year. It’s difficult though.” Alicia smiled at the little girl’s sigh.

"Yes, Rosa, but you have tried your best. You looked

after Steven. I think Father Christmas will reward you for being nice."

"Do you think I am nice?" Rosa asked, her big eyes studying Alicia intently.

"Of course I do; why would you ask?"

"Just curious." Rosa turned her attention back to Steven. Harry stared at her but he still wouldn't talk to her.

Alicia walked over to the window again but it was useless trying to see anything. The heavy snowfall blocked her view. She wondered if she should go out to look for Aaron but where would she go? She couldn't leave the three children alone. No, she had to wait for him to return.

"Come on children, let's play a game. It will make the time go faster."

"Will you tell us a story? We love them, don't we, Steven?"

Steven didn't answer but blinked twice. Rosa chuckled. "Steven said he likes your stories too."

Alicia settled the children in the bed and started telling them the stories. Soon they were fast asleep once more.

CHAPTER 30

She was dozing off by the fire when the door opened and Aaron arrived with two small animals. "I was going to skin them in the barn but it was so cold. I hope you don't mind."

Alicia gulped, hoping her stomach wouldn't disgrace her. They needed food and it wasn't as if they could pop to the store. She turned away as Aaron worked. The smell wasn't as bad as she feared. She watched as he set the meat to roast over the fire.

"Thank you. I have no idea what the children and I would have done if you hadn't come along when you did. I was worried something happened to you." She didn't look at him, not wanting to see his reaction to the fact she cared. He was getting married to someone else.

"It's been a long dry summer and now a cold

winter. The bigger animals are just as hungry as we are so food is scarce."

Wild animals? She looked around her as if they had just materialized.

"Sorry, Miss Carstairs." Aaron seemed to realize he had scared her. "I let my mouth run off sometimes. We are quite safe inside."

She hoped he was telling the truth.

"I heated up some of the leftover coffee. Would you like some?" She smiled at his shocked reaction. "I am not totally helpless, you know."

"I don't believe you are at all helpless." Aaron stared at her for a few seconds but she couldn't read his expression. Then he broke eye contact. "Yes, please. It's mighty cold outside."

"How long do you think it will be before they find us?"

"Won't be till morning now if we are lucky. No way the sheriff will risk any more folk in this weather."

"You mean we have to stay here all night?"

"Yes, ma'am."

"Oh."

"Guess I'll have to marry you now." Aaron's eyes sparkled.

Alicia's breath caught. "Why would you even think I would consider that, Mr. Higgins?" Alicia used her haughtiest tone, hoping it would hide her excitement at the idea of being his wife. *He isn't serious so don't go getting your hopes up.*

"Well, it won't do your reputation no good staying here all night with a strange man. The townsfolk will expect us to get wed." She glanced at him to see if she'd been wrong and he was serious, but she couldn't read anything from his expression.

"Marriage is a lifelong commitment. My reputation is already in pieces so thank you but no thanks." Her heart wanted more than anything else to say yes. But she wanted him to want to marry not feel obliged.

"Why?"

"Why won't I marry you?"

"No, why is your reputation in pieces? I ain't heard no one talking about you." Aaron stared at her but she couldn't meet his gaze.

"No? It's only a matter of time before you do. News travels fast in this world, especially bad news." She busied herself with the coffee.

"You want to talk about it?"

"No." She did but she couldn't bear it if he treated her differently.

"Okay then. Want to learn how to cook?"

Startled by his quick acceptance, Alicia allowed herself to look into his eyes. Big mistake. He smiled down at her.

"I emmm, well, I need to..."

"I tied a rope from here to the barn and outhouse. You best not stray too far from the rope. I don't want you getting lost again."

"I didn't get lost," Alicia started but stopped as he laughed. "You're teasing me, aren't you?"

"Yes, Miss Carstairs, I am. Go on be careful."

Cheeks burning, Alicia opened the door and headed out to take care of business. Embarrassed he knew exactly where she was going, she was also thankful he had made light of it. He was quite a nice man. Nice? *He's way more than that and you know it.*

CHAPTER 31

When she came back the children were wide awake. "I'm hungry and so are the boys," Rosa complained.

"Mr. Higgins is cooking us something to eat now. Doesn't it smell lovely?"

"What is it?" Rosa asked, her bottom lip quivering.

From what little time she had spent at the orphanage, she knew Rosa was sensitive about animals. She insisted various wild creatures were her pets. Alicia didn't want her to get upset about what they were eating. She decided to distract her.

"Rosa, why don't you tell us why you ran off?"

"Are we in trouble?" Tears brimmed in her big brown eyes.

"No, sweetheart, you are not in trouble. I am just sad you, Harry and Steven ran away."

"Harry wants to stay with his brother but the man said he had no use for Steven. Me and Steven love each other and we don't want to get separated."

Alicia hid a smile when Steven reached for Rosa's hand.

"What man?" Alicia looked at Harry willing him to answer her but the mutinous look on his face told her he wouldn't.

"Charlie Staunton said he'd adopt Harry but he wouldn't take Steven. He wasn't very nice. He said some horrible things."

Alicia clenched her hands into fists. She thought she had done enough to warn Charlie Staunton off. Obviously, she hadn't. No way was he going to adopt Harry. She would adopt both the brothers before she let them be separated. She'd find a way. "Charlie Staunton isn't adopting any children. We won't let that happen."

"Will you stop them separating me and Steven?" Rosa asked, her eyes full of tears.

"Why would anyone separate you? You will continue to live in the orphanage with Wilma, at least, until you are all adopted," Aaron said.

"Bertram said the orphanage was going to be turned into somewhere for white children only. He told me..." Rosa took a deep breath trying to speak through her tears. "John and I would be made to leave when Wilma goes."

Alicia couldn't talk as she was too angry.

"Where is Wilma going?" Aaron's confused tone matched the expression on his face.

"Bertram said she was heading to another town where they liked black people." Rosa swallowed hard. "Miss Carstairs, you're scaring me."

Alicia hadn't realized she was frowning. She forced her mouth into a smile and gave the little girl a hug. "Sorry, darling, I didn't mean to. Only I am very annoyed with young Mr. Shaw. How dare he spread vicious rumors like that."

"But you said whites belonged in their own orphanage with white minders and teachers. You know that first night you came with Steven and the other children," Rosa murmured, looking at the floor.

Shame coursed through Alicia's body. Her voice trembled as she tried to speak. Finally getting her vocal chords under control, she took Rosa's hand in one hand and lifted her chin with the other. "I was wrong to say that, Rosa. It was a wicked thing to say. I am very sorry I hurt you, John, Wilma and everyone else. I wish I could take back what I said."

The little girl stared at her in silence for a couple of seconds. "You really mean it?"

"Yes, I really do." Alicia tried to smile but her mouth was quivering as she held back the tears.

"Rosa, sweetheart, come here and give your uncle Aaron a big hug. Nobody is ever going to make you, John or any other child leave Clover Springs unless they want to go. I promise."

"What about Wilma?"

"Well, little lady, I guess a grown woman like Wilma has a mind of her own. But I don't think she wants to leave Clover Springs either. She loves the town and more importantly she loves all of you."

"So Bertram lied?" Rosa looked like she wanted to believe them but Bertram's lies had sunk in.

"I get the impression this child lies a lot," Alicia said. She wished she had young Mr. Shaw in front of her. She would teach him a lesson. *For sharing the same opinions, you did?*

As if he sensed her thoughts, Aaron spoke softly. "Children aren't born racists. They learn that behavior. Bertram seems to take better to that kind of learning than math and English. I will be having a word with him when I see him next."

Alicia knew she had to say something. Taking a deep breath, she bent down to the level of the children.

"I was racist too. I believed all those things people

said. I believed the rubbish printed in the paper. How could I have been so stupid?"

"You realize now you were mistaken. Takes a big person to admit when they are wrong." Aaron took her hand and pulled her to her feet. She pulled it away but not quickly enough to miss the look of hurt on his face. "Sorry. I'm sorry," she whispered but he had turned away.

CHAPTER 32

"Rosa, can you get some plates out of the cupboard, please." Aaron said, not looking at Alicia.

"I'll do it. Rosa, you stay next to Steven. I think he's getting a little cold."

Glad of something to do, Alicia pulled open the cupboard only to shriek as something moved inside.

Aaron was at her side in no time.

"What's wrong?"

"Th-theres something in there. I saw it move."

"Stand back. Could be a snake..."

Alicia took a couple of deep breaths. She watched as he opened the door carefully. He started laughing.

"What is it?"

"There's nothing in here other than a few spiders. They won't hurt you."

Alicia shivered, but it wasn't from her fear of spiders. His hand at her back made her pulse beat faster. She yearned to lean into him. Maybe he would give her a hug and then a kiss... *Alicia Carstairs. What are you thinking?*

Aaron put his hands on her shoulders and turned her to face him. Putting a finger under her chin, he gently forced her to look at him.

"I seriously doubt a few spiders scare you, Miss Alicia."

He leaned toward her, his eyes never leaving hers. He was allowing her to draw back if she wanted to. But she didn't. He placed his hand in hers, his fingers curling around hers sending a jolt through her. She allowed him to pull her closer, releasing his hand so he could slide both his arms around her waist.

She stared into his eyes, her knees trembling at the passion she saw darkening them. She couldn't believe he felt the same as she did. The thought left her breathless. She inched closer to him, wanting him to kiss her deeply. She didn't care who saw them. Nothing mattered but the man holding her. Her heart fluttered as his head came down to meet hers. His lips brushed hers gently before capturing them in a deep embrace.

* * *

He nearly growled with frustration when he heard the children giggling. He had forgotten they were there. He wanted to continue kissing her until her breath caught and her eyes glowed with desire.

His heart had turned over when he saw her lying on the ice trying to rescue Rosa. He was torn between wanting to kill her for being stupid and wanting to hug her for being so brave. He hadn't prayed so much in his life. Thankfully, his prayers had been answered and he had managed to get both off the ice before it shattered.

Seeing her here in his cabin, dressed in his old britches and a cotton shirt way too big for her, he'd realized how much he wanted her to stay. It was more than a sexual attraction, although her body felt like it was made for his.

He brushed her lips briefly once more before releasing her. Her flushed face made it even more difficult to let her go. He turned away to hide his physical reaction from the children and forced himself to think.

Could she make a life with him out here in the wild without the modern conveniences of the city? It was obvious she was educated and refined, words which would never apply to him. She was used to society life, the ballet and opera where he preferred the company of a few close friends.

Did she want to go back to live in Boston? If he cared for her, he would go with her. He shuddered at the thoughts of the city. All those people and noise, nowhere he could be alone with his thoughts. Lawrence's descriptions of society had illustrated a world where nobody cared about their neighbors. Ellen's and Katie's experiences were different, they had found a friend in their uncle's cook, but they had hated Boston too. He didn't enjoy visiting Denver so couldn't imagine how awful it would be to live in a bigger city. Would it be worse than living in Clover Springs if Alicia left?

But then hadn't she run away from Boston. Maybe she didn't want to go back there. Maybe, she would stay in Clover Springs. She'd become close to the children, proving today how much she loved them. His stomach churned again at the danger she had willingly placed herself in to rescue Rosa. Most people would try to rescue a child but it sure painted a whole different picture of the woman he had thought was heartless given the opinions she had expressed when she first arrived.

CHAPTER 33

Alicia slept in the bed with the children, Aaron on the floor in front of the fire. The next morning any hope of being able to return to Clover Springs was squashed. The snow covered everything in a deep white blanket and was still falling thick and fast. The children couldn't understand why they weren't allowed outside to play. But it was too cold and Aaron was worried they would wander off. Alicia and he worked hard keeping the children entertained. They sang Old Dan Tucker and Skip to my Lou until everyone was sick of them. They played Boston – Aaron called it Blind Man's Bluff. The children roared with laughter as a blindfolded Aaron tried to catch them. Alicia stood in front of the fire watching as she didn't want anyone getting hurt. She suspected Aaron may have cheated as he grabbed her and swung her around several times.

"Miss Alicia owes me a prize as I caught her. Don't you agree?"

Rosa suggested she repay Aaron with a kiss while Steven laughed. Harry didn't join in. Alicia gave in and kissed Aaron on the cheek. Just as she leaned toward him, he moved so she ended up kissing him on the lips. The children clapped as Alicia's cheeks turned bright red.

The hours passed quickly, but despite having fun, the children fretted about not being able to go home.

Aaron kept them supplied with fresh water by going out in the snow every day with a shovel and breaking the ice in the creek. Sometimes he managed to catch some fish which were a welcome treat compared to the beans and tinned peaches they had in the house. He hadn't been able to catch any meat since that first evening.

Alicia boiled some water to give the children a quick wash. Aaron had forgotten about the tin bath he had stored in the barn until Rosa complained that the boys stank. They didn't have enough water to fill it up properly but it was enough to give Rosa, Harry and Steven a rub down.

Alicia reckoned the adults could do with a bath but

she was too shy to suggest having one. It wasn't as if Aaron and the boys could wait outside.

* * *

IN THE EVENINGS, they settled around the fire telling stories. Aaron was surprised to find Alicia enjoyed his sense of humor and laughed at his jokes. She was quite funny too. She had always been so quiet and aloof at the orphanage but out here in the middle of nowhere, she seemed to bloom. He couldn't help wishing they could stay forever. Rosa missed Wilma dreadfully but the boys seemed happier in the homestead. Harry didn't speak to Alicia but he spent time listening to her stories. Alicia had told him about the incident on the train and how she wished Harry would forgive her. Aaron sensed the young boy was warming to Alicia.

He found himself looking forward to the evening when the children were in bed asleep and he was left alone with Alicia. She told him stories of her early life in Boston. He could have listened to her speak for a year. He wasn't much interested in big cities but he loved her accent. He found himself getting annoyed over the amount of times her mother seemed to put her down, but as she didn't seem to realize what she had said, he didn't comment on it. He knew not everyone had a ma as decent as his.

He tried asking about her life just prior to her being on the train but she closed up. The expression of sadness in her eyes was so heartbreaking he changed the subject determined never to be the one to subject her to pain.

He told her of his past, about the Indian attack in which his pa had died. How he loved and respected his ma. He told her about buying the homestead and how important it was for him to be self-sufficient. Not reliant on anyone else including the Sullivans.

"I thought Mary and Davey were your friends. They seem like lovely people." Alicia said, her face showing surprise at his comments.

"Don't misunderstand me. They are the best. I just don't want to live off other people. Does that make sense? I have my pride."

They talked of all sorts of things but neither of them mentioned the future. He wished he could ask her to stay in Clover Springs but was that fair? She was used to city life, maybe she should go back to Boston. Father Molloy was bound to have friends in the city who could help her.

CHAPTER 34

"Look at us, we are like an old married couple with the children in bed and us sitting here in front of the fire." He watched her reaction closely but couldn't tell what she was thinking. He was about to ask her to consider staying when she surprised him.

"You will be an old married man in a little while." She stared at the fire.

His heart leapt but fell just as fast as she continued. "When is your mail order bride arriving?"

How did she know about that? Embarrassed he stood up.

"Don't know. Look at the woodpile. It's getting low. I best get some more as the fire will go out overnight otherwise. Night, Alicia."

He almost ran out the door. He didn't want to think about his mail order bride. The only woman he wanted was sitting at his fire.

* * *

THE NEXT DAY, the snow was again too deep to leave. The children were bored and fed up singing and playing games. They kept asking what was going to happen when they got back to Clover Springs.

"Will we be sent back to Boston if they can't find families to take us?" Harry asked. Steven moved closer to his brother and Rosa sat up on Aaron's lap.

"I am sure Father Molloy and the rest of the townsfolk will do everything to let you stay in Clover Springs."

"Father Molloy will make sure you and Steven are adopted together," Alicia said, although Aaron noticed her fingers were crossed.

"How do you know?" Harry's rude tone upset Aaron.

"Harry, show some respect. Do not speak to Miss Alicia like that. Apologize now."

"Sorry!"

Although the boy apologized, the look in his eyes showed he was anything but. It wasn't the time to discipline him. They were all getting fractious waiting for the weather to clear. He put the children to bed early and told them a story. Alicia went to kiss them goodnight as usual but Harry turned his face away.

Aaron wanted to hug Alicia and tell her everything would be fine but the expression on her face stopped him. Instead, he poured some coffee and handed it to her. She took a seat as usual by the fire.

"Alicia, don't let Harry upset you. He is just reacting to what nearly happened to Steven. He's been through a lot these past months."

Alicia sighed. "No, he hates me and he's right. What do I know? I can't give them a home or make sure someone adopts them both."

"Would you like to adopt them?" Aaron watched her reaction carefully.

"Who is going to let me? I have no husband, no job and no money. Not exactly the best prospect, am I?"

Before he could say anything, she excused herself and went to bed leaving him staring into the fire.

Would she consider marrying him? That night he dreamt Alicia was his wife and the two boys their sons.

* * *

THE NEXT MORNING, he was determined to ask her that evening if she would stay in Clover Springs. He spent the whole day humming and singing. He caught her glancing at him a couple of times but she didn't say anything. She looked a bit pale. She's sick of being stuck indoors too. He guessed she missed going riding. He had been so jealous when she went riding so often with Little Beaver even though his friend was happily married. Why couldn't he see his feelings for what they were?

Despite his good humor the day seemed to drag. The children weren't interested in going to bed. Eventually, he had to bribe them with two stories and a quick game of Old Mother Wobble. He had balanced on his head for a few minutes to make them laugh and promised to play a longer game the following day.

Finally, the children fell asleep and he took his seat by the fire. He had to ask her now or he would lose his nerve. He looked into her face. She was staring into the fire, her cheeks flushed with heat.

"Alicia, have you…"

"Sorry, what did you say?"

"Alicia, are you feeling alright?"

"I'm fine. Just a bit tired," She managed before she fell sideways. He caught her easily and carried her over to the bed. He woke the children so they'd move over to let her lie down. Her skin was burning with a fever. She had caught a chill.

CHAPTER 35

"Is Miss Alicia going to die?" Rosa asked, her lower lip trembling. The child had put his fears into words but he couldn't let her know that. "No, little lady, we will make her better." He hoped he sounded more confident than he felt.

He sponged her down gently. He hoped it would be enough. If his ma or any of the women from town were here, they would know what to do. There was a reason men left nursing to women, it came easier to them.

She thrashed about on the bed, kicking the covers from her body one minute, clawing them back over herself the next.

Morning came and she wasn't any better. He kept the children fed but Alicia wouldn't eat. She was barely drinking. He knew he should be seeing some improvement by now but if anything, she was getting worse.

"Is Miss Alicia getting better?" Rosa asked, removing her thumb from her mouth to talk. "She don't look too good."

"It's just the fever, Rosa. It will break soon and then Miss Alicia will be back to normal. She just needs to rest a little. Will you help me look after her?"

Rosa's brown eyes stared up at him as she resumed sucking her thumb. Slowly she nodded her head.

"Good girl. You keep this cloth on her forehead. It will help cool her down. She may push it off so just keep putting it back on again. I'm going to get some ice."

"You gonna give her an ice bath?"

Aaron flushed at the question. He didn't want to do it but Alicia's temperature was still rising. It might be her only chance.

"Yes, Rosa, I think I am." He moved toward the door leaving Rosa talking to Alicia. The two boys sat near the fire, their slumped shoulders echoing his feelings. She had to get well. She just had to.

"Miss Alicia, you got to fight to get better. Mr. Aaron, he's got to give you an ice bath. It's ever so cold."

But Alicia didn't answer. She just lay there, her

chest rasping as she struggled to breath. Rosa's tears fell on her face but there was no reaction.

"Mr. Aaron, you best get that ice bath ready real quick."

Aaron didn't answer. He knew the young girl was right. He only hoped it would help Alicia recover.

As he made his way outside, he looked at the sky. Despite the blizzards of the last few days, the sky seemed loaded with snow. If only Alicia was well enough to ride, then they could try to make it to Clover Springs before the next snow hit. But there was no way he could manage the woman as well as the children. Maybe the townsfolk would find them. Hopefully, they would bring the doc or at least Emer or Mrs. Grey with them.

* * *

ALICIA SHUDDERED as the cold pierced her senses. She struggled but her limbs wouldn't obey her. Her mind seemed to be outside her body, as if this was all happening to someone else. She heard a child crying but couldn't drag up the energy to open her eyes. She just wanted to sleep.

"Alicia, come on, darling. You got to fight harder. You can't give in now. I won't let you." The voice penetrated her brain. She recognized it but couldn't remember his name. He sounded like he cared about her. Was it Robert? Her fiancé. No, he didn't want her. He wanted to take her to Mr. Oaks. She didn't want to go. *No Robert,* she croaked before she slipped into darkness once more.

* * *

"WHO'S ROBERT?" Rosa asked.

"I don't know," Aaron snapped. Seeing the child's face, Aaron immediately apologized. "Sorry, little lady, I didn't mean to shout."

"You are just worried about Miss Alicia. I know that." She smiled up at him making him feel worse. Alicia calling out another man's name hurt but it wasn't going to stop him doing everything he could to make her better.

* * *

ALICIA OPENED her eyes and immediately wished she hadn't. Every part of her body ached and she couldn't remember ever being so weak.

"Mr. Aaron, Miss Alicia's awake now. Look," Rosa said excitedly.

"Looks like the ice bath did the trick and broke

your fever. You need to rest a bit more but you should recover quickly."

His smile was gentle but his eyes looked pained. She wondered why but didn't have the energy to think about it now. She lay back, closing her eyes once more.

Sometime later, she woke up. Nobody noticed. She lay in bed watching him as he spoke to the children. He was so gentle with them. He stood up to check whatever was cooking on the fire. She closed her eyes quickly not wanting to be caught staring at him. She kept them shut as his shadow crossed her.

"Miss Alicia, it's time for you to eat something. We got to build your strength up."

Alicia opened her eyes catching him smiling at her. Her heart flipped. She smiled back but his smile disappeared, it was as if she had imagined it.

"Can you sit up? Rosa will help you eat."

Rosa crawled onto the bed beside her.

"I can manage," she said but her voice came out as a weak whine.

"You've been really ill, Miss Alicia. You got to let us get you better so we can go home. It's Christmas Eve tomorrow."

Christmas Eve already. That meant they had been in the cabin for almost a week. In that time, he had washed and cared for her like a newborn babe. Her cheeks flushed as she realized just how intimate they had been. She burrowed under the covers as if behaving modestly now would have any impact. She was ruined. No respectable man would consider making her his wife now. Not after she had spent a week unsupervised with a man who wasn't her husband or a family member.

"Eat."

His command sounded almost like a shout. She opened her mouth as Rosa fed her. She didn't know what had happened but something had changed. Aaron wouldn't look at her and seemed angry. She sensed it was more than just being cooped up in a small cabin with a sick woman and three children. She wished she could ask him what was wrong but the presence of the three children stopped any chance of private conversation. *Or kissing.*

CHAPTER 36

Christmas Eve dawned and for once it wasn't snowing. The sky was clear and blue.

Aaron came into the house stamping his feet to clear the snow off his boots. "Come on, children, let's get you home to Clover Springs."

Rosa and the boys screamed in excitement and chattered nonstop about going home. Alicia tried to share their enthusiasm but she didn't want to leave. She wanted to stay here with Aaron and pretend they were one family. She wanted him to kiss her again and hold her tight, although that was a big wish given he was barely talking to her. She couldn't figure out what she had done wrong and there hadn't been a chance to ask. It was almost like he was avoiding being alone with her.

He helped her mount the horse but let her go so

suddenly she nearly fell off. He muttered an apology but didn't look at her. It was the same when he helped Rosa up in front. He held Steven in front of him with Harry hanging onto his back. The horses were eager to get moving too. They must have been fed up being inside too.

* * *

When they pulled up outside the orphanage, there was nobody about. Aaron dismounted with the boys before helping Rosa down from Alicia's horse. Finally, he turned to her, putting his arms around her waist to lift her down. Her skin shivered at his touch. She smiled hoping he would smile back but he didn't even look at her. She opened her mouth to say something but happy shrieks from the orphanage interrupted.

"You are back. Thank the Lord. We were so worried about you." Ellen flew over to them kissing Aaron before kissing Alicia. "We knew Aaron would find you and the children and keep you safe until the beastly weather broke. Come inside. Everyone is here. We are getting ready for Christmas."

Alicia followed reluctantly. She desperately wanted to speak to Aaron but he took the horses to the barn.

. . .

SHE SMILED as John gathered his sister in his arms and rocked her. Both had tears running down their faces. The other children welcomed Harry and Steven back and pulled them in to see the tree.

* * *

"DO YOU LIKE THE TREE, Miss Alicia?"

"It's beautiful, Wilma." Alicia forced herself to look happy, although her heart was breaking. She followed Wilma into the kitchen.

"Mrs. H showed Laura and the other ladies how to crochet snowflakes for the tree. Sorcha, who hates sewing of any kind, helped the children string and make paper decorations. Mrs. H. and I baked sugar cookies and gingersnaps in different shapes with the intention of using them as decorations."

"They were so delicious they were disappearing as fast as they were coming out of the oven." Ellen laughed. "You'll be lucky to find one on the tree."

"Miss Carstairs, are you sure you are happy to be back?" Rosa asked looking up at her. Alicia picked Rosa up and twirled her in the air as the young girl giggled and shrieked. "Its Christmas Eve, everyone should be happy tonight."

Alicia set Rosa back down carefully, catching Harry watching her closely. Any efforts she had made at conversation in the homestead were rebuffed. She supposed she should wait for him to make the first move but then she was the adult and he the child. She'd been in the wrong and he'd been quite right to correct her.

"Would you like me to help you put your decoration on the tree, Harry?"

"You've changed. You are much nicer than you were on the train."

"Harry, don't be rude to Miss Carstairs," Ellen scolded before Alicia touched her on the arm. She leaned down to Harry's level. "I behaved very badly on the train. Do you forgive me?"

Harry's response was to throw his arms around her neck. "Thank you for saving Steven."

Alicia laughed loudly as she hugged the little boy closer. "I guess I am forgiven." She exchanged a smile with Ellen over the boy's shoulder.

* * *

"Mr. Aaron, he say you been ill. He's gone to see his ma. He said you got to go to bed and I got to give you my chicken soup."

Her smile faded as she realized Aaron had left without saying goodbye.

"Don't fuss please, Wilma, I wasn't that sick."

"Yes she was, Miss Wilma. She was so sick Mr. Aaron had to give her a bath in ice. It was ever so cold." Harry flinched as if remembering.

Alicia wished she could disappear. All eyes in the room seemed to be looking at her. Was it concern over her being sick or the fact a man who wasn't related to her had given her a bath? She couldn't tell and to be honest, now he'd gone, she didn't care.

"Get yourself up them stairs. I is going to give you a warm bath and put you to bed. I don't want any argument about it."

Alicia was going to protest that she wasn't a child but one look at Wilma's face and she decided she best do as she was told.

The bath helped and despite fretting about Aaron, she did sleep.

CHAPTER 37

The next morning, Rosa came to wake her to tell her everyone was going to church. She dressed carefully hoping he would be there.

Her heart leapt in her chest as she spotted him waiting at the church door. "Merry Christmas, Aaron," she said softly. She had to stop herself crying out at his response. "Miss Alicia."

He wandered over to Samuel and she found herself standing alone at the door. Taking her seat in the church with Harry and Steven on either side of her, she wished she had a veil to cover her face. Gulping back the tears, she cuddled the boys as she tried to concentrate on the service but it passed in a blur. Her gaze kept drifting to Aaron sitting ahead of them. Why had he changed toward her? She thought he cared as much as she did. Maybe he'd realized she wouldn't make a useful wife. But that couldn't make him act so distant. He was behaving as if they had only exchanged a couple of words not lived together for over a week. He'd given her a bath for goodness sake. As well as kissing her. Her breath quickened as she remembered his kiss. She shouldn't be thinking about that in church. But where had the intimacy that had grown between them prior to her getting ill gone?

* * *

AARON WAS tired having tossed and turned all night. Surely she wouldn't have kissed him back if she loved another. She looked so beautiful this morning but the sadness was back in her eyes. Was that because of him? He had to speak to her. Maybe just ask her who Robert was and if she loved him. He waited impatiently for Reverend Timmons to finish before he exited the church. He would wait for her outside.

She came out the door shortly after him but before he could move, a stranger moved to greet her.

"Thank goodness you are safe and well. I was so worried about you."

"Robert, what are you doing here?" In Alicia's confused state, she spoke quite loudly.

Aaron stiffened. Robert. The name she had murmured when she was ill. He stared at the pompous stranger. He might be tall and handsome but he had an ugly sneer on his face rather than a smile. He couldn't imagine what it was about him Alicia found attractive. Maybe he was very wealthy.

"I am here to get married. Did you hit your head? Has your memory failed you? We agreed to be married on New Year's Eve. When you went missing, I had to hire a detective to find you. You led us a merry dance from Denver to Leadville. It wasn't until we met a lady who remembered you on the train with a priest we could track you to Clover Springs. We can catch up on the train. We have to get back to Boston."

Aaron hated Robert's whiny voice. He sounded annoyed rather than relieved to find his fiancée safe and well. Still it had nothing to do with him. Alicia was a grown woman and she obviously had feelings for this man.

"Isn't it romantic? Imagine having a man chase you around the country." Ida Hawthorn sighed dramatically. Was she fluttering her eyelashes at Robert? Women!

Aaron turned to leave. This was none of his business.

"Robert, there is nothing wrong with my brain, my head or indeed my memory. We were engaged but you broke off that engagement back in Boston. Months ago, it was on your recommendation I travel to Leadville to take up employment with Mr. Oak."

Robert scowled as he took her arm. Aaron didn't like the way his fingernails bit into the flesh on her arm. He took a step forward when he saw Alicia had tried to move away but Robert tightened his grip.

"You must have been injured, Alicia, you are obviously confused. I never broke off our engagement. Why would I do something so dreadful. I loved you. I still love you. Why else have I spent months trying to track you down? After you disappeared I was beside myself. But I refused to listen to the rumors."

"What rumors?" Alicia asked, trying to remove his hand.

"That you ran off with a manservant."

Alicia laughed, but Aaron knew she wasn't amused. "Me run off with Mr. Bates? As if anyone could make the aged butler run anywhere."

* * *

ALICIA STOOD STARING AT ROBERT, he was hurting her arm. She knew what had happened in Boston. She just didn't understand why he had changed his mind. Why did he suddenly want them to get married? He wasn't in love with her. She didn't have much experience with affairs of the heart but he could barely look at her.

"Robert, I am sorry you were concerned and for your wasted journey. But I won't be marrying you," she said stiffly as she wrenched free of his grasp. Wilma moved to her side, her gaze fixed on Robert's face. Alicia couldn't help feeling relieved. If Wilma sensed there was something wrong, too, it wasn't just her being overwrought.

"Oh, yes you will." Robert's tone was barely civil. "We had an agreement to get married, one enforceable by law. If you don't agree to the marriage I will sue you for breach of contract."

Now she did laugh. "Sue away. I don't own anything of any value. You, above all others, know how my financial situation was left after...what happened in Boston." Too late she remembered they had an audience.

"When your father murdered your mother and then killed himself."

The shock reverberated through the crowd. Alicia's knees trembled as she willed herself not to let anyone see what effect his words had on her.

"That's enough. Whatever business you have with Miss Alicia should be conducted in private not in view of anybody who cares to listen. She deserves more consideration than that," Aaron said decisively. Alicia sent him a quick look of gratitude but he was staring at Robert.

"What would you know about what she deserves?" Robert sneered.

"Miss Carstairs and Mr. Higgins just spent a week together. Unchaperoned." Miss Hawthorn sighed dramatically as she moved closer to Robert. Alicia would have laughed at Ida's interest in Robert had she not wanted to throttle her.

"It was hardly planned that way and with three children in tow. After seeing Miss Carstairs saving the lives of those children with no thought of her own safety I can vouch for her character. Speaking of the children, they don't need to witness any nasty confrontation. Ellen, could you take them back to the orphanage please. Miss Carstairs could also do with a lie down, she has been very ill."

"Harry, Steven, go with Miss Ellen. I will follow later." Alicia shooed the children off with Ellen. Wilma took her arm lending her some strength. She sagged against the other woman thanking her with a squeeze of her arm.

"I do not see that this is of anyone's business but mine and Alicia's."

"I don't agree. As I said before, I think there is something peculiar going on here. Miss Carstairs is not capable of acting in the manner you suggest."

Alicia wanted to run into Aaron's arms as he kept defending her.

"You know her, how long? About a month, yet you presume to know her better than someone who grew up with her, was considered by her father to be as close as a son. Our marriage was a foregone conclusion for many years."

"I may not know her as long as you but I think I know the real person. Her actions of the last week do not match those of the fly-by-night person you speak of. I suggest, sir, you take the train back from wherever you came. As Miss Carstairs has pointed out, you have had a wasted journey."

"I intend to marry my fiancée and nobody is going to stop me."

Alicia realized she had to do something. "I can't marry you, Robert. I am going to marry Mr. Higgins. I must as I may...well, I could be carrying his child."

Alicia faltered over the last words, not believing they had come out of her mouth. Something about Robert scared her. In desperation to get away from having a future with him, she had just told the town the man she did love was a bounder.

CHAPTER 38

Alicia opened her mouth to apologize to Aaron but the words wouldn't come. He held her gaze, his eyes glued to her face. She couldn't read his expression. What would he do now? Would he tell the town the truth? He had never touched her? Or would he save her?

"Let's take this conversation somewhere more private. Mrs. Timmons won't mind us using her sitting room. Alicia, follow me. Aaron, you must come too. You, sir, I have not yet made up my mind what role you play in this picture but perhaps you best come along too. Reverend Timmons, fetch Father Molloy. I think we could all do with your combined council." "Yes, Mrs. Grey"

"The rest of you, get along with your own business. There is nothing to be seen here. "

The crowd didn't disperse but they did make way for Mrs. Grey to lead the way to the Timmons' home. Wilma held onto Alicia's arm as if she would never let go. Alicia was glad as her legs were very wobbly. She desperately wanted to go back to the orphanage and hide in her room in shame. What had she been thinking? Accusing Aaron publicly wasn't going to endear herself to him.

Father Molloy arrived shortly afterwards with an official looking man.

"Miss Carstairs, my name is Perceval Wilkenham. I am a US Marshal investigating the circumstances of your parents' deaths."

Alicia couldn't believe it. First Robert and now a US Marshal. What a Christmas this was turning out to be.

"Sorry, Mr. Wilkenham, but I believe that matter was already investigated. I was told my father murdered my mother before he turned the gun on himself."

"Yes, I am afraid that is what the police first thought. Someone made it look that way."

Alicia sat down with an unladylike thud. "Do you mean...?"

"We believe your father was murdered as well. We do not believe he killed your mother but was, in fact, also a victim of the same person or persons."

"But why? Why would anyone want to kill my parents? Why would they make it look like he killed her? He adored her."

"We believe they did so to cover their tracks."

Alicia swayed. Aaron moved quickly to hold her hand.

"Don't you think Miss Carstairs has been through enough? She became very ill after rescuing the children from the creek. She has yet to recover her strength. First, she had to deal with him turning up, and now you with this story. It's enough for anyone never mind a vulnerable young woman."

"Quite right too. Please take your questions and leave, Mr. Wilkenham. My fiancée has no wish to hear about her parents any more. The whole episode was too painful," Robert added staring pointedly at Aaron holding Alicia's hand.

"Why do you think they were murdered? Alicia's asked, her voice trembling.

"Your father's law firm was involved in some very shady business dealings." Mr. Wilkenham said.

"I can't believe my father would have condoned anyone breaking the law. But then he owed all those people money."

"We are not at all certain your father was aware of what was happening. Your father was ill, Miss Carstairs."

Alicia nodded. "He'd been having headaches for a while."

"Those headaches were caused by a growth on his brain. The doctors had told him he had months to live. Your parents didn't want to tell you. They wanted to spare you for as long as they could. But his condition meant he was becoming more confused. So, he had passed a significant amount of control in his business over to the person he trusted."

Alicia turned on Robert. "You. My father trusted you with everything. You were like the son he never had."

"Exactly, Alicia, that's why I couldn't understand when you ran away. All your parents wanted was for us to get married."

"Father tried to tell me something. He gave me the family bible and told me never to let it out of my sight. He suggested I go stay with my mother's family. I didn't want to. I didn't know them. I wanted to stay in Boston with the people I loved. I thought he and Mother wanted to get rid of me." Alicia looked into the faces of those around her before staring at Robert. "I was wrong. They were trying to protect me." Her voice broke on the last word.

"We believe your father did become suspicious and those suspicions probably lead to his death."

"But who killed him? And why kill Mother too?

She wasn't involved in the business." Alicia's voice rose. Aaron let Alicia's hand go.

"It was you, wasn't it?" Aaron grabbed Robert by the arm.

"Me. How dare you? Is it not bad enough you keep an innocent young woman out in the middle of nowhere without throwing accusations like that at my character?"

A punch on the nose made Robert shut up rather quickly.

"Thank you, Mr. Higgins, but perhaps you would leave the detective work to me. All leads have led to Mr. Venebles but unless he confesses, we don't have any evidence of guilt."

"Alicia, your bible. Maybe your father put something in it," Mrs. Grey said quietly.

Father Molloy stood. "I believe I may be able to fill in some of the blanks for your investigation. We have been concerned about Mr. Oaks and his friends for a while now. Perhaps you and I can sit and discuss this in more detail. Wilma, take Miss Carstairs home and put her to bed. She needs some rest." Father Molloy's tone showed he expected to be obeyed without question.

"Aaron, take this...*gentleman* to the sheriff. He can lock him up until we get to the bottom of this mess."

Alicia stood, her limbs shaking badly. She leaned against Wilma taking strength from the other woman.

"You go to bed now, child. Wilma will look after you. Don't worry about anything. You have a home here in Clover Springs. We look after our own." Mrs. Grey gave her a quick hug before turning to Father Molloy. "I will go to the orphanage and get that bible, Father."

"Come along, Miss Alicia. Time you was in bed. You listen to old Wilma now. You don't look strong enough to take a deep breath let alone deal with this now. Nothing happening here that can't wait another day or two."

Alicia looked toward Aaron but he was staring out the window. She wished she had the courage to say something to him, but what? Holding her head down, trying to keep the tears from flowing, she let Wilma lead her out of the house and back toward the orphanage.

CHAPTER 39

Alicia paced back and forth. The news her parents had been murdered was a shock. How could she have believed all the bad things said about her father? Wilma had held her while she cried before telling her it was partly her parents' fault. They hadn't wanted to hurt her by telling her about Papa's illness so his strange behavior went unexplained.

Upsetting as the news about her parents was, it was the way she had treated Aaron that caused her to pace. She couldn't believe she'd told almost the entire town she might be pregnant. She didn't care about her reputation which was in tatters anyway but Aaron was a good man. The best. He deserved better.

"Miss Alicia, you have a visitor."

"Tell Robert to go away, please, Wilma."

"Sheriff won't let that man out of the jailhouse.

Seems he knows about some of that stuff Father Molloy was talking about. It's Mr. Aaron done want to speak to you."

Aaron was here. She glanced in the mirror. There was nothing she could do about the tear stains. She gave her cheeks a good pinch and almost ran down the stairs.

"You two can talk in the kitchen. I reckon you got a lot to discuss." Wilma walked off, laughing softly.

"Aaron, I'm sorry. I…"

"Alicia, be quiet and listen to me. Are you in love with Robert?"

"What? Of course not. What made you think that?"

"You called his name when you were sick."

A glimmer of hope made Alicia step closer to Aaron. "I was dreaming he had come to take me away." She inched closer. It was now or never. "From you."

Aaron looked at her, his expression one of disbelief.

"Aaron, I am in love with you," she whispered.

"Me?" His face lit up.

"You." She reached up to kiss him. He swung her into his arms before kissing her deeply. She was breathing heavily when they finally broke apart.

"Well, I guess we best get wed then. Especially as you might be having my baby."

She gasped. "Aaron, I'm so sorry. I panicked and didn't know how to get rid of Robert."

"I forgive you so long as you promise it is something we can prove to be true, soon." He was teasing her again.

"Aaron," she muttered, trying to be embarrassed.

He held her and kissed her again showing her exactly how he felt.

"Speaking of children, do you mind if we start married life with children."

Puzzled she waited for him to explain.

"I thought we might adopt the boys, Harry and Steven."

She shouted for joy before kissing him hard. Her shout brought the adults and children running.

"What's going on now?" Wilma demanded, her hands on her hips.

"We're getting married and having sons." Aaron answered before kissing Alicia again.

"Miss Alicia, you is having a baby?" Wilma looked horrified.

Both Aaron and Alicia laughed.

"No, Wilma," Alicia answered but at the same time Aaron said. "Not yet." They grinned at each other until Wilma coughed.

"Harry, Steven, how would you like Miss Alicia and I to adopt you?"

"You mean be our ma and pa?"

Everyone looked at Steven.

"You can speak."

Steven smiled as Alicia gathered him in a hug. Harry joined in followed by Aaron.

"I guess the answer is yes."

"Well, you didn't actually ask me yet," Alicia teased but her smile said yes.

Father Molloy chose that moment to come into the orphanage closely followed by Mrs. Grey and Mr. Wilkenham.

"Alicia, we need to speak with you. In private."

Alicia paled, her hand reaching for Aaron's.

"I want Aaron to stay."

The priest nodded as everyone else left the room.

CHAPTER 40

"Alicia, your father left a letter in the bible. It was hidden in one of the pages."

"I couldn't look in it. I found it too painful." Alicia said quietly.

"It helps to explain everything. Your father suspected Mr. Venebles and his friends were up to something. He regretted telling him about his illness and worried for your safety. He must have known his own life was in danger." Father Molloy's gaze was full of pity.

"Poor Papa." Alicia choked, glad Aaron had taken her hand.

"I wish he had gone to the marshal with his suspicions."

Father Molloy coughed and they all fell silent. "It turns out Mr. Venebles has been involved with Mr.

Oaks and his associates for quite some time. He owes them a significant amount of money and they were blackmailing him into organizing various business transactions. Your father tried to stop Mr. Venebles who appears to have panicked and killed both your parents. He couldn't kill you so he..."

"Decided to send me off to Mr. Oaks instead." Alicia shuddered. Aaron held her hand tighter under the table.

"Well, yes. Thank goodness we met on the train."

"But why did Robert come back? Surely he should have stayed away."

"That was the part that puzzled me as well until we realized that your father owned a gold mine."

"Papa did? He never said anything."

"The deed is in the bible with this letter. Mr. Venebles found out, how we aren't sure. Anyway, greed overcame wisdom and here we all are."

"He wanted the money not me." Alicia said.

"You are a very wealthy young woman, Miss Carstairs," Mr. Wilkenham explained.

Aaron released her hand and pushed back his chair. "I will leave you to discuss this."

"No, Aaron, wait. I want you to be here."

Aaron looked at her but shook his head and left. She went to follow but Mr. Wilkenham stood up blocking her exit. "If you will excuse me, Miss Carstairs, but I need to get back to Boston. There is a good chance we can catch the rest of the people involved in this criminal ring. Your ex-fiancé has become quite cooperative."

"Amazing what some will do to save their own neck," Mrs. Grey said, her tone telling everyone what she thought of Robert.

"What will happen to Robert? Will everyone find out my parents were innocent?" Alicia asked Mr. Wilkenham.

"Yes, Miss Carstairs. Your father's reputation will be fully restored."

"Thank you, Mr. Wilkenham."

The marshal nodded. Aaron offered to show him out.

"Alicia, we found your father's will. He..."

Alicia stood up as it was apparent Aaron wasn't coming back in. "Sorry, Father Molloy, please excuse me. I want Aaron to come back and listen to this."

She moved quickly not wanting Aaron to disappear. She found him by the barn.

"Aaron, please come back inside. Father Molloy wants to read us something. Papa's will."

"No, Alicia, can't you see? Things have changed. You are a very rich woman. You now have enough money to live wherever you wish."

“I want to live here. The money doesn’t matter,” She insisted but he wasn’t listening to her.

“But it should.”

“Why?”

“It just should.”

He was a stubborn man. She may love him but she didn’t like this side of his character. She had to bite down her temper, though, and tread carefully or she would lose him forever. She couldn’t bear that.

“Aaron, if we never found out about the money, would you still be telling me I shouldn’t stay with you?”

Aaron didn’t answer. She took a chance and moved closer to him.

"Would you?" She whispered.

"No. But it doesn’t matter what may have happened. Fact is you're rich."

"We are rich. Once we are married, it will belong to you."

"I don’t want any of it."

"Are you telling me I have to choose between the money and you?"

Again, no answer.

"I guess that’s my answer." Alicia grabbed his hand and pulled him after her as she made her way back into the house.

“What are you doing, Alicia?”

"I want you to listen to me talk to Father Molloy. Please. Just this once."

Aaron shrugged but followed her into the kitchen where Father Molloy and Mrs. Grey sat talking. They stopped as the couple walked in.

CHAPTER 41

"I would like to give the mine and all of its gold to the orphanage. Can I do that?" Alicia asked. "Does the will allow it?"

"Well... It is certainly a generous gesture but..."

"Alicia, you can't do this," Aaron protested.

"It's my money. I think I can do with it what I please," Alicia snapped. "I want everyone paid back – all those people who lost their money. I would like to restore my father's good name. But I don't want anything from the mine."

"But what will you do? You don't have an income," Mrs. Grey asked. Alicia couldn't be sure but she thought she saw approval in the older woman's eyes. It made her brave.

"I would like to stay here in Clover Springs and adopt Harry and Steven just as I planned," she said.

She hoped Aaron would say something but he stayed silent.

"But, Alicia, you know you cannot adopt as a single lady." Father Molloy looked confused.

"I won't be single. Will I, Aaron?" Alicia bit her lip as she looked at him waiting.

He stared at her for a couple of seconds before drawing her into his arms. "Are you sure about this?"

"Absolutely."

"But I cannot give you anything."

She kissed him lightly on the lips. "You have already given me everything I need. A home, a family and your love. I don't need anything else," Alicia insisted.

"While I admire your spirit, Alicia, I suggest you reconsider your thoughts. Having children is an expensive business. It would be to both your benefit to start life with a little financial cushion. Don't you agree, Mrs. Grey?"

"Certainly, Father. While I appreciate the sentiment behind Alicia's actions, I believe she is being less than prudent. Then there is always the matter of her father's wishes."

Alicia made a sound of protest.

"Your father did everything he could to protect you, Alicia. The least you can do is try to abide by his wishes. He suggested the assets be held in trust until such a time as you are thirty or married for twelve months. Whichever comes first. "

"Oh, you mean we have to keep it?" Alicia gazed at Aaron but he stared at Mrs. Grey.

"You can make a decision on your first wedding anniversary. For now, you can pay off your father's creditors and take a small allowance. I am sure you could convince the trustees to make a financial contribution to the orphanage. After all, it has provided you with food and lodgings for the last few months."

"The extra money would certainly help the children," Father Molloy said, his eyes showing he was trying hard to remain serious.

Alicia bit at the side of her finger. What should she do now? She didn't want to lose Aaron, yet she couldn't give away the money. Her hands were tied.

"Aaron?" she asked, her voice hesitant. "I know it's not what you want but I would give it away if I could."

Aaron stayed silent. Alicia's heart beat so loud she thought the whole room could hear it. She wanted to move into his arms but she had to let him make his decision.

"I think you are amazing, and I will be the luckiest man alive when you become Mrs. Higgins."

He drew her toward him and gave her a deep kiss. Father Molloy coughed causing Mrs. Grey to laugh.

"Perhaps we best get the wedding arranged tout de suite." Mrs. Grey muttered drawing Father Molloy from the room, closing the door behind her.

Aaron pushed the hair back from Alicia's forehead before gently kissing her.

"I can't believe you would have given all that money up just for me."

"I would." She sighed as he kissed her once more. "Although…"

"hmmm…"

"Well, the homestead could benefit from indoor plumbing and the boys will need horses and…."

Aaron burst out laughing. "I think, Miss Carstairs, you are not totally prepared to leave your old life behind in Boston."

She smiled at him. "I think you could be right. I would live with you anywhere, Aaron, you know that, don't you?" He nodded. "But it would be nicer to live in some comfort."

Putting his hands around her waist he twirled her in the air. "Anything you want, fair lady, just so long as you say you will be mine. Forever."

"Yes, please," she murmured before pulling his head to hers and kissing him deeply.

EPILOGUE

"You nervous, Miss Alicia?" Wilma took the brush from her hands and started brushing her hair. "Only natural to be on the day you be getting married. Mr. Aaron, he be a fine man. He'll treat you right."

"Wilma, why do you call everyone Miss and Mr?" Alicia asked softly, she didn't want to upset Wilma but her curiosity got the better of her.

"Not sure what you mean, Miss Alicia?" Wilma didn't look up but kept her eyes focused on the brush.

Alicia reached out to take the brush, her eyes meeting Wilma's in the mirror. Alicia turned around without losing her grip of Wilma's hand.

"You are no longer a slave."

"That be right. I be free a long time."

"Yes, you are free and you are also my equal so why not call me Alicia?"

'I don't think that be fittin." Wilma started to brush her hair once more.

"My friends call me Alicia. I thought we were friends. I know I was horrible when I first came to Clover Springs but I've changed. You, Mrs. Grey, the ladies, Aaron, Little Beaver and everyone else made me realize how wrong I was. Rosa and Harry pushed me to accept the truth." Alicia gulped. "I love the boys so much, Wilma. Rosa too. I can't believe Harry and Steven are going to come home with me tomorrow."

"Oh, they ain't going home with you tomorrow."

Alicia felt the color drain from her face.

"No, Mr. Aaron, he don't want to be sharing your company tomorrow night with anyone never mind two children." Wilma giggled like a school girl. "The children be staying here for a few days. To give you and Mr. Aaron time to…talk." Wilma's eyes gleamed. "Miss… I mean, Alicia, you should done see your face. You the color of milk, girl."

"Wilma! You scared me." Alicia's face flushed as the implication of Wilma's words sank in.

"That's better. A nice rosy red suits you nicer than the color of milk." Wilma couldn't stop laughing. Alicia smiled at her via the mirror.

"You are beautiful, Alicia. You always was on the outside, but now your inner beauty is a match."

Alicia spun around to wrap her arms around Wilma. "Thank you for everything, Wilma. I wouldn't have changed without your love and friendship."

"Don't you sell yourself short. Your heart was big enough to change, miss… Alicia. I don't know if I ever going to get used to calling you by your name."

"Well, I ain't going to answer to no miss anymore." Alicia's almost word perfect imitation of Wilma's accent had them both laughing hard.

"I sure is going to miss you and those young'uns." Wilma said after they both stopped laughing. "Now young Steven found his voice, he never knows when to stop talking."

"I never thought I would be this lucky. I have a man who loves me and two new children. A perfect family. I got everything I wanted for Christmas and a whole lot more besides." Alicia smiled happily.

"The magic of Clover Springs works all year around, Alicia, not just at Christmas."

"What was the blessing Father Molloy said on Christmas morning? You know after he said the prayers."

"'The light of the Christmas Star to you

The warmth of home and hearth to you

The cheer and goodwill of friendship to you

The hope of a child like heart to you
The joy of a thousand angels to you
The love of the son and God's peace to you.'"

Wilma said softly, her eyes glistening with tears.

"I have been blessed so many times since I came to Clover Springs. Everyone has. You will be too. You, Aaron and your new family. You'll have your hard times, we all got those. But keep that blessing in your mind and good times won't be far away."

Wilma gave Alicia a quick hug. "Now you best be getting dressed or Mr. Aaron will think you done run away."

"Stay with me please, Wilma. Walk with me to the church."

"You try stopping me."

ABOUT THE AUTHOR

Rachel Wesson is a USA Today Bestseller and author of several series including a number set against the backdrop of World War II. Having always been a fan of history, Rachel tries to combine her love of history with a good story.

Rachel Wesson was born in Kilkenny, Ireland but considers herself to be from the capital, Dublin as that's where she spent most of her life. Her dad brought Rachel and her two sisters out every Saturday to give their mother a break. He took them to the library and for ice-cream after. It took a long time for her sisters to forgive her for the hours she spent choosing her books!

She grew up driving everyone nuts asking them questions about what they did during the War or what side they were on in the 1916 rising etc. Finally her Granny told her to write her stories down so people would get the pleasure of reading them. In fact what Granny meant was everyone would get some peace while Rachel was busy writing!

When not writing, or annoying relatives, Rachel

was reading. Her report cards from school commented on her love of reading especially when she should have been learning. Seems you can't read Great Expectations in Maths.

After a doomed love affair and an unpleasant bank raid during which she defended herself with a tea tray, she headed to London for a couple of years. (There is a reason she doesn't write romance!). She never intended staying but a chance meeting with the man of her dreams put paid to any return to Ireland. Having spent most of her career in the City, she decided something was missing. Working in the City is great but it's a young person's dream. Having three children you never see isn't good for anyone. So she packed in the job and started writing. Thanks to her amazing readers, that writing turned into a career far more exciting and rewarding than any other.

Rachel lives in Surrey with her husband and three children, two boys and a girl. When not reading, writing or watching films for "research" purposes, Rachel likes to hang out with her family. She also travels regularly back home – in fact she should have shares in BA and Aerlingus.

ALSO BY RACHEL WESSON

The Resistance Sisters

Darkness Falls

Light Rises

Hearts at War

When's Mummy Coming

A Mother's Promise

WWII Irish Stand Alone

Stolen from her Mother

Orphans of Hope House

Home for unloved Orphans (Orphans of Hope House 1)

Baby on the Doorstep (Orphans of Hope House 2)

Women and War

Gracie under Fire

Penny's Secret Mission

Molly's Flight

Hearts on the Rails

Orphan Train Escape

Orphan Train Trials

Orphan Train Christmas

Orphan Train Tragedy

Orphan Train Strike

Orphan Train Disaster

Trail of Hearts - Oregon Trail Series

Oregon Bound (book 1)

Oregon Dreams (book 2)

Oregon Destiny (book 3)

Oregon Discovery (book 4)

Oregon Disaster (book 5)

12 Days of Christmas - co -authored series.

The Maid - book 8

Clover Springs Mail Order Brides

Katie (Book 1)

Mary (Book 2)

Sorcha (Book 3)

Emer (Book 4)

Laura (Book 5)

Ellen (Book 6)

Thanksgiving in Clover Springs (book 7)

Christmas in Clover Springs (book8)

Erin (Book 9)

Eleanor (book 10)

Cathy (book 11)

Mrs. Grey

Clover Springs East

New York Bound (book 1)

New York Storm (book 2)

New York Hope (book 3)

Printed in Great Britain
by Amazon

39735766R00142